Squaw Hunters

Brogan McNally was a drifter who somehow always ended up with trouble on his hands. Perhaps it was because he was a sucker for the hard-luck story!

Venturing into California he was horrified to stumble on the headless bodies of ten Indians. Soon he would learn that a bounty was being paid for each Indian head and, once again, he was determined to help the underdogs.

He had to face some mighty tough hombres with fast-gun reputations, but Brogan himself was no slouch with a gun. His deadly skills would finally bring justice and peace to the land, but not before much blood flowed.

By the same author

The Ghost Riders
Brogan: Passing Through
Brogan's Mexican Stand-off
Luther's Quest
Brogan for Sheriff
Brogan: Fool's Gold
Brogan and the Bull
Zeke and the Bounty Hunter
Brogan: Shepherd's Gold
A Town Called Zero
Brogan Takes Toll
Thirteen Days
Brogan: To Earn a Dollar
Brogan and the Judge Killer
Brogan: Kidnapped
Caleb the Preacher
Brogan: Blood Money
Pioche Vendetta
The Hunter Hunted
Gringo
Maverick
Black Day in No-Name
Riverdale Showdown
Double Take
The Bullfrog Trail
Pitiquito Trail
Grizzly
Storm Over Gold Rock
Destination Seminole

Squaw Hunters

L.D. TETLOW

North Lanarkshire Council Motherwell Library Hamilton Road Motherwell	
7 77O242 47	
Askews	25.6.01
	£10.50
COA	1094800

A Black Horse Western

ROBERT HALE · LONDON

© L.D. Tetlow 2001
First published in Great Britain 2001

ISBN 0 7090 6842 5

Robert Hale Limited
Clerkenwell House
Clerkenwell Green
London EC1R 0HT

The right of L.D. Tetlow to be identified as
author of this work has been asserted by him
in accordance with the Copyright, Designs and
Patents Act 1988.

Typeset by
Derek Doyle & Associates, Liverpool.
Printed and bound in Great Britain by
Antony Rowe Limited, Wiltshire

ONE

The distant fire was obviously a big one and under normal circumstances Brogan McNally, saddle-tramp, would have avoided it since fires usually meant trouble and he was not looking for trouble. At first he wondered if it was a forest fire, but it appeared too localized for that and he decided that it must be a building or buildings. Such fires were, in his experience, better avoided.

On this occasion however, despite looking hard for another way round, he had very little option but to keep on riding towards the thick plume of smoke. The mountains either side of him were far too high and steep to climb and the only way through seemed to be directly along the valley towards the fire. He estimated that it was about three or four miles ahead and he did not rush himself to reach the spot.

In situations such as this caution played a very big part in his actions since the last thing he wanted was to become embroiled in other folks' troubles. At least that was always what he told himself. The reality very often proved quite different. Unfortunately for him very often, Brogan McNally was a sucker for a hard luck story. Even his many years of drifting had not cured him.

When he did eventually arrive at the scene, he stopped short and surveyed the area for some time but there did not appear to be anyone around. Cautiously he approached the rather ramshackle array of buildings, most of which were now burned to the ground. He also discovered things which perhaps he might have been better off not discovering for his own peace of mind.

The first grisly sight to greet him was the spread-eagled body of what was obviously an Indian man. The man's general colouring and clothing on the body told him that much, but positive identification was quite impossible simply because the man had been decapitated. Strangely and quite bizarrely, there was no sign of his head. He very quickly discovered nine more bodies, again all obviously Indian men and once again all had been decapitated – but their heads were nowhere to be seen, although he did not look too hard.

He had seen massacres of Indians and even white folk before from time to time, but this was the first time he had come across a massacre where the heads of the victims had been deliberately removed and apparently taken away.

He cautiously picked his way through the charred remains when suddenly his gun was in his hand. He had not heard anything definite, but he knew that someone was watching him. He stopped, looked and listened and eventually made his way towards the one loose-boarded building which was still standing. He circled the building twice before dismounting and, very slowly and with extreme caution, went towards the door.

'Better come out with your hands raised!' he

commanded. 'I know somebody's in there.' The only response was a slight sound from inside. It may have been slight and brief but the noise confirmed his feelings. 'Come on out, I said,' he shouted again. 'It's OK, I don't mean you no harm.' Once again there was no response. 'OK, I'm comin' in!' he called, at the same time kicking the door open and immediately flattening himself against a wall. The expected volley of shots did not materialize and, after a few moments Brogan almost threw himself into the building, gun in hand, ready to use it if necessary.

Having established in his own mind that the headless bodies outside were Indians, the sight which greeted him was not entirely unexpected. The light from the doorway lit up a scene of terrified hopelessness as what appeared to be about a dozen Indian women stared at him, cowering closely together and obviously expecting to be gunned down. For a few minutes they stared at each other until Brogan finally slipped his Colt into his holster and withdrew. He sat on a small barrel and waited.

After about five minutes two figures appeared in the doorway. The one had the typically weather-beaten and lined face of an elderly Indian woman, but the other was a young man, probably in his late teens or early twenties. They both looked at Brogan for a few moments, mistrust and fear in the eyes of the woman but the youth seemed a little more certain of himself, even slightly arrogant. Slowly he approached Brogan.

'What happened?' asked Brogan, nodding in the direction of one of the headless bodies. 'It must've been one hell of a party you had.'

'Men from Cottonwood come,' replied the youth in very good English. 'You are white, you must know what these men from Cottonwood do.'

'Son,' said Brogan, sitting up straight, which had the effect of making both of them take one step backwards and the youth to grab at a knife in his belt. 'I ain't never heard of this Cottonwood place, let alone know what the men from there do or don't do. An' don't get no ideas about usin' that knife. A bullet is a whole lot faster than any knife.'

'You are not from Cottonwood?' queried the youth, replacing his knife and smiling thinly.

'I don't even know where it is,' asserted Brogan. 'Now what happened here? Mind, if you don't want to tell me that's fine by me. I'll just keep on ridin' an' forget everythin' I've seen.' The youth and the woman remained silent. 'Fine,' Brogan eventually sighed. 'It's none of my business I guess. I'll be on my way.' He stood up and went towards his horse.

'They call themselves Squaw Hunters,' the youth suddenly said. 'The men from Cottonwood, they call themselves the Squaw Hunters. You have never heard of these men? You must know, everyone knows what they do.'

'No, son,' replied Brogan. 'Not everyone. I don't. Mind, that's not too surprisin' I guess since I don't come from these parts. As a matter of fact I don't even know which state I'm in.'

'California,' said the youth. 'This is the state known as California.'

'California,' mused Brogan. 'Maybe I should've guessed, I knew I was pretty close. OK, since I asked, what the hell did happen here an' just who are these Squaw Hunters an' who owns this farm?'

'The farm belongs to my people,' replied the youth. 'We are Lakota. The men from Cottonwood who call themselves Squaw Hunters come this morning. They come many times before but always we are ready and our women, girls and children are led into the hills. Sometimes they burn our farm, sometimes they do not. This morning they come, five of them, this time they take us by surprise. As you see, they kill ten of our men. Then they take as many women and girls as they please. Some of the younger girls are raped many times. I even see two of our small boys taken by these men.'

'Don't you have guns to fight back?' asked Brogan.

The youth reached into the building and produced an ancient muzzle-loading rifle.

'Only these,' he said. 'They are of little use against men with modern guns.'

'I'll buy that,' agreed Brogan. 'But why cut off their heads an' what have they done with them? I don't see any lyin' about.'

The youth smiled ruefully. 'In Shasta City one Lakota head is worth five dollars and nobody asks how the head was obtained.' By that time most of the other women and a couple of youths had come out of the building, all dressed in a mixture of rather tattered western dress and traditional Indian dress. They stared sullenly at Brogan, fear and mistrust still in their faces. 'You see no small children and no horses,' continued the youth. 'They were all taken away by the Squaw Hunters. The children too are worth many dollars when they are sold in Shasta or Cottonwood. The horses are either sold or butchered.'

'Sold!' exclaimed Brogan. 'That's slavery. You must have it wrong son, slavery has been abolished. It's against the law.'

'They do not call it slavery,' replied the youth with a derisory smile. 'I do not know how it is they can do these things but as far as any Indians are concerned there is no law.'

'What about the state authorities?' said Brogan, 'Ain't none of you told them what's goin' on?'

The youth laughed loudly. 'It is plain to see that you do not come from these parts otherwise you would know. It is these very authorities who make it possible for our women to be raped, our men murdered and for our children to be sold as slaves. There is nobody for the likes of us to complain to.'

'I reckon you must have it wrong, son,' said Brogan. 'Nobody can do what I've just witnessed an' get away with it.'

'Go to Shasta City or Cottonwood and you will soon discover the truth,' said the youth.

'Which is nearest?' asked Brogan.

'Cottonwood,' replied the youth. 'It is perhaps two days.'

'Then I guess that's where I'll go,' said Brogan. 'I need some supplies. I'll make sure someone hears about what happened out here.'

'And they will laugh at you,' said the youth. 'In California an Indian is considered as less than the droppings of a pig.'

'Maybe they will, maybe they won't,' said Brogan. 'At least I'll make sure somebody hears about this. What's your name, boy?'

'It is better if nobody knows,' said the youth. 'I have had the misfortune to have been educated by the missionaries and have returned to my people. The men from Cottonwood and Shasta do not like such as I who have been educated but have returned to the old ways.'

'I'd hardly call livin' on a farm the old ways,' said Brogan.

'It is true,' the youth smiled ruefully. 'For most, the old ways have gone, the white man has seen to that. There are still a few who retain the old ways, living in the hills but they are hunted and killed. It will not be long before there are none alive who know the old ways.'

'Will they be back, the men from Cottonwood?' asked Brogan.

The youth shrugged. 'Who can tell? Sometimes they do not come for many months. Sometimes they come every week for many weeks. Always they seek the same thing. Women to satisfy their lust, children they can sell and the heads of men to take to Shasta.'

'Then why don't you do somethin' about it?'

'If we fight we are branded as renegades and many men, even soldiers, come to kill us,' replied the youth. 'If we complain we are ignored or even killed for complaining.'

'I see,' said Brogan, not quite sure if he believed what he was hearing. The young man seemed genuine enough and Brogan was inclined to believe that at least *he* believed it. 'Well, I guess there's nothin' I can do here. I reckon you'll want to bury your dead or whatever you do with them. If there's nothin' I can do, I'll be on my way.'

'There is nothing you can do,' said the youth. 'I fear that there is nothing anyone can do for us now. The white man has destroyed our way of life and most of my people are now strangers in their own lands.'

'What will you do?' asked Brogan.

'I will lead those of us who are left into the hills to join others already there,' said the youth. 'At least in the hills and forests we stand some chance of surviving. I know those men, they will return, I know it, and next time they will kill everyone they find. Had they found me and the other two young men this time we would now be dead and our heads removed.'

Brogan shook his head in disbelief. He was well aware that Indians were considered akin to vermin in some parts of the country, but he had never come across anything like this. Whilst the killing of an Indian was probably not treated too harshly by the authorities elsewhere, at least the killers were usually subject to some form of justice in the form of a fine or short term of imprisonment.

'Good luck,' said Brogan eventually. 'It sure looks like you're goin' to need it.'

'We thank you for your concern,' said the youth. 'There are others in Cottonwood and Shasta who think as you do, but they have no voice. A word of warning. There are some of my people and other tribes who have joined with the white man. They are known as Indian Police and are used to track us down. They are hated by my people even more than the white man and will do almost anything, including killing white men who stand in their way.'

'I'll remember that,' said Brogan. 'I still reckon you must have got things wrong though.'

'You will soon learn,' said the youth. 'You will learn the truth and then you will forget all about us.'

*

It might have been a two-day journey to Cottonwood for a man travelling at normal speed, but Brogan and his horse rarely travelled at normal speed. As far as Brogan was concerned time and place held little meaning. With nowhere in particular to go and the remainder of his life in which to get there, an extra day or even week here or there usually meant nothing. It took them the remainder of that day and then almost three days to reach the town.

At first glance, Cottonwood was no different from thousands of other towns. It was larger than some but smaller than others. It appeared to consist of one main street and four or five side-streets. Most of the houses were little more than shacks along with some very grand-looking dwellings at one end of the town, which was not unusual. There were the normal stores and shops such as a bakery, hardware, general store, drapery shop, bootmaker, gunsmith, two hotels and three saloons and a few others. What industry there was seemed confined to a lumber mill on the edge of town. There was also a railroad station and an area of livestock corrals.

As he rode down the main street, the only thing which struck him was the total lack of interest in him. In most towns further inland, a stranger always attracted a great deal of interest and very often a hostile greeting from the local sheriff who would take one look at him, realize that he was a saddle-tramp, and immediately suggest that his visit be as brief as possible. A deputy sheriff walking along the boardwalk hardly seemed to notice him.

There were two livery stables, one of which advertised feed at fifty cents and appeared a little more run-down than the other. This was the one Brogan chose. For his part the owner hardly blinked when Brogan suggested that he might be allowed to bed down with his horse for the night. He did, however, charge an extra fifty cents for the privilege. There were rooming-houses in the town, he had seen at least three, but they were establishments he always avoided. He had spent most of his life in the open air and did not feel comfortable in a bed. A pile of straw was the height of luxury as far as he was concerned.

After seeing to his horse and secreting his precious rifle in some nearby straw, Brogan made his way along the street to a seedy-looking eating-house he had seen. The food, however, belied its surroundings and was really very good.

The eating-house was run by a large woman who had the unfortunate habit of sniffing loudly and wiping her nose on the sleeve of her dress at regular intervals. Brogan took the opportunity to ask questions about the Indians. However, he was not at all surprised by her response.

'Ain't nobody gives a shit about no Indians,' she sniffed. 'Only good Indian is a dead one as far as I'm concerned. My man was murdered by them a couple of years back. Why you askin'?'

'On my way here I came across a farm owned by some Indians,' he told her. 'At least they claimed to own it. The farm had been burned down, ten men had been murdered and apparently some children taken. They told me the children were to be sold as slaves.'

'There ain't no such thing as murder when it

comes to Indians an' slavery's against the law,' said the woman. 'Everyone knows that, includin' them Indians. Although they seem to think the law don't apply to them.'

'Then why should they say it?' asked Brogan.

'On account of they want to cause trouble, that's all,' she replied. 'Either that or they gets confused. I think they deliberately act confused when it suits 'em, hopin' folk'll take pity on 'em.'

'So there's no such thing as slavery?' said Brogan. 'Why should anyone want to take the children then? They seemed pretty certain about it. That ain't the kind of thing people make up stories about.'

The woman looked at him with a scornful expression. 'Mister, I wouldn't believe a damn thing any Indian told me. You ain't one of them do-gooder religious men, are you? We gets a few through here from time to time. They soon learn though an' they don't stay.'

'Do I look like a religious man?' asked Brogan.

'You sure don't smell like one,' she sniffed. 'Most men round here smell like a good bath wouldn't hurt but you smell worse'n most.'

'I am very religious when it comes to soap an' water,' said Brogan with a large grin. 'It's against my religion to use the stuff. So what's this I hear about there bein' a bounty on Indian heads of five dollars?'

'That ain't here,' she huffed. 'They say that's out at Shasta City. I suppose they told you about that? I heard about it but I don't believe it. I reckon it's just another of them tales put about by the Indians.'

'Seems to me it's more'n a tale,' said Brogan. 'There were ten bodies of Indian men, all of them had had their heads removed an' there was no sign of them. I can't see nobody removin' heads just for the hell of it or to make a good story. Why should they? They didn't know I was around.'

'Don't know nothin' about that,' she said. 'I ain't the person to ask. Maybe you'd better speak to Sheriff Max Ford. Then again, maybe it'd be better if you just forgot everythin' you've seen or been told for your own sake. Max Ford don't like it when folks start askin' too many questions, especially strangers who don't know how things are in these parts.'

Brogan thought about it for some time and eventually but somewhat reluctantly, decided that since it was really none of his business, he might as well keep quiet. He already sensed that he would meet a wall of either silence, prevarication or even downright hostility. He also knew that the fact that he was a saddletramp would certainly not endear him to those in authority. Much as he might have sympathized with the plight of the Indians, common sense told him that the situation was far too big for the likes of him to become involved. The young Indian had been right; he would learn the truth and then forget all about it.

He needed a few supplies and spent a couple of hours gathering them. He was tempted to ask the owners of the stores about what had happened to the Indians but what he thought was his better judgement prevailed.

There was a good sprinkling of sorry-looking Indians around the town, most sitting dejectedly and staring empty-eyed into space or taking surreptitious drinks from bottles when they thought nobody was looking. There were also quite a number of Indian children all, apparently, working for those in business. In form they looked like children but all seemed lost and lifeless. Old eyes set in young heads, looking yet seeing nothing, younger versions of the older Indians on the streets.

The one thing he did learn was that timber, hunting for furs and some gold prospecting were the chief occupations of the citizens of Cottonwood. There were also, apparently, a few farms and a couple of ranches out of town. Once again, he was somewhat surprised at the almost total lack of interest in him. It struck him that Cottonwood was a town which probably had a constant stream of people like himself passing through but rarely staying. There seemed little reason for anyone to stay.

That lack of interest even extended to the saloon he entered. Very often it was in the saloons where his presence was challenged, usually by someone intent on making a name for themselves by proving that they were a better gunfighter than the next man or simply because he was what he was and, like the Indians of Cottonwood, saddletramps were often considered fair game. Actually he found the situation somewhat unsettling, but it did make a change to be able to go about his business unchallenged.

He was approached by several bar girls who actually appeared somewhat relieved when he declined their invitations, although one did swear at him. He also found himself standing next to a man wearing the badge of office of a sheriff. This was obviously Sheriff Max Ford.

The sheriff sniffed and looked hard at him for a few moments but said nothing directly to him.

Instead he made loud comments to a man on his other side about the air suddenly becoming too thick to stay any longer. Brogan simply smiled and finished his drink. Having had enough, he, too, wandered out into the dark street.

He was in time to witness a group of eight Indian children varying in age from about three or four years to about twelve being ushered along the street and eventually led into a a small shack. The woman herding them shouted something at them and finally locked them inside. Brogan wondered if these were the children the young man claimed had been taken from the farm. However, he made no attempt to find out.

A short time after the children had been locked away, two deputy sheriffs and two Indian men who wore some sort of uniform similar to army uniforms, walked slowly along the street, the two deputies on one side and the two uniformed Indians on the other. Brogan assumed that the Indians were members of the Indian police the young man had mentioned.

The targets of the deputies and the Indian police were obviously those other Indians who, apparently, dared to still be out. Most simply got to their feet as the four officials approached and, unsteadily, made their way to various tumbledown hovels. The few who did not move fast enough were helped on their way by savage kicks or felt the weight of rifles slamming into their backs or even heads. The two Indian policemen appeared the more aggressive.

Brogan found the process quite fascinating and watched for quite some time. Eventually the four men returned, the two deputies crossing the street towards Brogan and the two Indians disappearing down a side-street.

'What was all that about?' Brogan asked casually as the deputies came towards him.

'Curfew,' grunted one of the deputies, looking hard at Brogan. 'Ain't no Indians or blacks allowed on the streets after nine.'

'Blacks! I don't see no blacks,' said Brogan.

'That's 'cos there ain't none,' said the other deputy. 'If there was they'd have to be off the street too. What's it to you, mister?'

'Nothin', I guess,' said Brogan. 'Just curious.'

'It don't pay to be curious,' said the first deputy, looking hard at Brogan again. 'Ain't you the feller what was in Grace Higgins' diner earlier on?' Brogan nodded. 'Yeh, she told me about you. She said you was askin' too many questions. She said somethin' about you bein' out at the Lakota farm an' findin' Indians with their heads cut off.'

'I was,' agreed Brogan. 'Ten Indian men, all with their heads missin'. It just seemed kinda strange to me, that's all.'

'You plannin' on stayin' long?' asked the other deputy.

'As long as it takes,' replied Brogan.

'That ain't no kind of answer,' grunted the first deputy. 'Take my advice, get your ass out of here as soon as you can.'

'Now that's the kind of greetin' I'm more used to,' said Brogan, laughing. 'I was beginning to wonder why nobody was takin' an interest in me.'

'Just get your ass out of here,' grated the deputy. 'Or it might just be that you could be spendin' the night in jail. We charge five dollars a night an' that don't include food.'

Under different circumstances Brogan might well have goaded the deputies further, but he simply laughed and shrugged before wandering off towards the livery stable. He was not looking for trouble, but then he rarely looked for trouble, it just sort of happened. He was aware of the deputies watching him as he crossed the street but they did not trouble him further. However, he had the feeling that it would be wise to take their advice and leave Cottonwood at the earliest opportunity.

TWO

Brogan spent a peaceful night in the livery stable, his only complaint being that the ticks seemed rather more plentiful and aggressive than normal. On waking, the first thing he did was to light a cheroot and spend almost half an hour removing the ticks with the lighted end. This was the only really certain method of removing them. Simply pulling them off usually resulted on the heads being left attached to the skin and, if allowed to remain, they often festered.

When he eventually emerged into the daylight he found the town strangely quiet. There appeared to be only three stores open for business, the remainder still had their shutters up. At first this puzzled him but was explained when he asked the owner of the bakery, one of the three, why everything was so quiet.

'Because it's Sunday,' explained the baker. Not for the first time, Brogan had lost track of what day it was. Which particular day of the week it happened to be was not something that he considered important, one day was much the same as any other as far as he was concerned. 'Most places is closed on Sundays,' continued the baker. 'All decent folk will be in church at ten an' then they'll be goin' down to the auction. Everybody needs bread, that's why I open, but apart from me the only other stores open belong to a coupla Jews – they'd open all night if they thought it'd earn 'em an extra dollar. The saloons open their doors at midday, after the auction, an' that's where most of the men head for.'

'Auction?' queried Brogan. 'What auction?'

The baker laughed. 'We call it the livestock auction or the meat market. It happens every few weeks or so. Folk come in from the outlyin' farms an' the ranches when the meat market is on. Stranger round here ain't you?' Brogan nodded. 'You just go along, follow the crowd, you'll soon find out what it's all about.'

'Maybe I will,' said Brogan. 'I ain't got much else to do. You say everywhere is closed. How about the eatin'-houses? I'm hungry.'

'All closed,' said the baker. 'Grace opens up about four o'clock but the other two stay closed all day. If'n your hungry the best thing you can do is buy somethin' here. I got bread, butter an' cheese. It ain't much but it sure is better'n goin' hungry.'

'Maybe I'd better,' agreed Brogan.

He bought a small loaf, a quarter of butter and half a pound of cheese, which he took back to the livery where he sat next to his horse and consumed his meal. The bread was still hot and, whilst it tasted very good, he quickly discovered that it tended to come back on him. He also purchased another bag of feed for his horse before wandering back into the street where he sat beneath a large tree and watched as the faithful of Cottonwood trooped to church.

The service lasted just over an hour and, as predicted by the baker, almost everyone went off in the direction of the livestock pens. Brogan had no interest in livestock but, for the want of something better to do, he tagged along behind the crowd. He was very surprised to discover all the pens completely empty, but that did not seem to deter the crowd. It was obvious that something was about to happen so he waited.

What did happen took him completely by surprise, although on reflection he ought to have expected it. The group of children he had seen the previous night were ushered into one of the pens, the large woman who had been with them now forming them into a line according to size. Six fully grown Indian men were also herded into an adjoining pen. The term *livestock auction* suddenly took on new meaning and Brogan found it difficult to believe what he was seeing.

A large, well-dressed man and an elderly Indian man suddenly entered the pen containing the children and the well-dressed man proceeded to address the crowd.

'Ladies and gentlemen,' he boomed. 'Today we have eight children, all of sound limb and all guaranteed good workers. There are five boys and three girls . . .'

'Can you guarantee the girls are still virgins?' demanded a voice in the crowd.

'Of course,' responded the well-dressed man, who was apparently the auctioneer. 'I do not deal in soiled goods. I have my reputation to consider.'

'That's what you said last time,' replied the voice.

'I bought a ten-year-old an' when I got her home I found out she wasn't a virgin. How old are these three an' this time, if I decide to buy, I want a guarantee or my money back.'

'I can assure you the girl you bought had not been tampered with by anyone here,' replied the auctioneer. 'I can't speak for what happened to them among their own people. These girls are about ten or eleven years old, I can't say more'n that, it's almost impossible to tell exactly as you know. You are, of course, at liberty to examine them before you purchase. Billy Running Horse here...' he indicated the aged Indian to his right, 'guarantees that he is their legal guardian and as such has the authority to offer them for sale. I am prepared to start off the bidding for the girls at seventy five dollars apiece....'

Brogan could hold his tongue no longer. 'I thought slavery had been abolished,' he called out. The entire crowd turned and stared at him and for the first time he noticed that the minister from the church was amongst them. 'Ain't that so, Reveren'?' he called to the minister. 'Slavery is against the law.' Brogan was suddenly aware of the sheriff and two deputies closing in on him. The auctioneer, athough plainly taken aback by Brogan's outburst, very quickly recovered his composure.

'Ladies and gentlemen,' he called. 'It seems that we have amongst us someone who has a misguided impression of exactly what is happening here.' By that time the three law officers had surrounded Brogan and were about to drag him away. 'Please, Sheriff,' said the auctioneer. 'Allow me to enlighten our friend.' The three men relaxed their grip on

Brogan. 'Obviously you are a stranger to these parts, my friend,' continued the auctioneer. 'It is true, slavery has been abolished and is against the law. However, in the State of California and, for all I know, in other states, there is legal provision for children of any colour to be sold as apprentices – providing the permission of a guardian or other suitably qualified person is obtained. In this instance Billy Running Horse, in the absence of their parents, is their guardian.'

'That's 'cos their parents have probably been murdered,' said Brogan. 'I believe these children were taken on a raid on their farm. In fact I was at that farm just after they were taken.' He turned and looked hard at the crowd and the minister in particular. 'Ten Indian men were butchered, their heads had been cut off. I hear that Indian heads fetch five dollars apiece in Shasta City an' maybe in other places for all I know.'

'This is not Shasta City and we do not pay for the heads or scalps of Indians,' responded the minister. 'I do not doubt that you did come across such a scene, it is not unusual. Indians are savages and it is common for them to butcher each other. It is a well-known fact that they even eat their own children. What we are doing here is an act of Christian charity. We are saving the souls of innocent children by removing them from the source of such barbarity and bringing them into God's good grace. They are placed with good families who will ensure that that they are well treated, well fed and receive a good, Christian upbringing, thus saving their souls from everlasting torment in Hell's fires.'

'Bullshit!' rasped Brogan. The minister looked

suitably shocked at this remark and the sheriff and the deputies tightened their grip on him. 'That farm was attacked by some men from Cottonwood who call themselves the Squaw Hunters.'

'My friend,' called the auctioneer. 'What else would you expect those Indians to say? They will protect their own no matter what they do to each other. What is easier than to blame what happened on the white man as far as they are concerned? The Reverend Stowell is quite right. It is our Christian duty to save the souls of these children.'

'What about those six men?' demanded Brogan. 'I don't think you could claim you are saving their souls.'

'Not that I have any need to explain the law as it applies in California to anyone,' said the auctioneer, 'but I will. These men are classified as vagrants. They have no money and no obvious means of support. The law states that such men – or women – must pay their way in society by submitting themselves to four months' indentured service. At the end of that service they are freed. Now, ladies and gentlemen, having enlightened our friend on certain aspects of the law, we shall continue with the auction. . . .'

'An' we'll talk more about this in my office,' hissed Sheriff Max Ford. 'Come on, mister, an' don't try to make any trouble. Maybe you'd better hand over that gun of yours just in case.'

Brogan did not need to hand the gun over, it was suddenly withdrawn from his holster by one of the deputies. He recognized both deputies as those he had confronted the previous night. The last thing Brogan saw of the auction as he was led away, was several prospective buyers examining the children very closely, looking at their teeth, eyes and even genitals as they might any other animal.

Sheriff Max Ford looked at Brogan with obvious distaste from the safety of the opposite side of a large desk. He picked up the Colt taken off Brogan and examined it closely. Eventually he laid it to one side and grunted.

'Nice piece,' he said. 'How come a man like you can afford such a weapon? I reckon you must've stolen it off somebody.'

'I ain't never stole nothin' in my life,' said Brogan, rather proudly. 'I bought that gun fair an' square.'

The sheriff looked scornfully and then smiled. 'You got saddlebum written all over you an' you sure smell a whole lot worse'n even most saddlebums I ever met. Since when did any saddlebum never steal anythin'?'

'I can't speak for others,' said Brogan, 'but this is one saddletramp what's proud to be called a saddletramp. I ain't never stole nothin' off nobody in my life. I ain't never raped no woman, I ain't never been arrested for no crime.'

'Like you said to the Reveren' Stowell, bullshit!' said the sheriff. He sat back in his chair and looked Brogan up and down for a while. 'I gotta admit that there's somethin' about you what don't sit too easy in my mind. Every other saddlebum I ever met is shit scared of his own shadow, only too ready to lie through his teeth, but from what I've seen an' heard of you, you don't seem scared of nothin'. Either you really ain't scared or you is very foolish or you is lookin' to end your life pretty damned quick.'

'We all act foolishly from time to time, Sheriff,' said Brogan, 'Even you ought to know that. . . .' Max

Ford looked sharply at Brogan but said nothing. 'As for lookin' to end my life pretty damned quick, that's somethin' I never look for. I figure it'll happen one day but I ain't over anxious to know just when.'

'Which just leaves you not bein' scared,' said the sheriff. 'Yeh, I seen quite a few gunfighters in my time too. There's somethin' about the way you wear your gun which tells me you also know how to use it.'

'I ain't no gunfighter,' said Brogan. 'You got it right first time when you said I was a saddlebum.'

'Not a gunfighter,' mused the sheriff. 'Mister, when I look into those eyes of yours I know enough not to want to challenge you to a fight. I'm reckoned to be pretty good with both handgun and rifle but I have me this feelin' that I wouldn't even get my pistol out of its holster before you gunned me down. OK, I can almost believe that you ain't never stole nothin', but I don't believe that you ain't never murdered nobody.'

'You'd better believe it,' said Brogan, casually picking his gun off the desk and slipping it into his holster. 'Sure, I've killed my share of men, probably more than most of your regular gunfighters. I don't deny that. What I do deny is that I have ever murdered anybody. Murder is against the law an' believe me or not, as you choose, I ain't never broken the law either. Every man I've ever killed either deserved it or I killed them in self-defence. I don't tell lies either an' that includes what I saw out at that Indian farm, the one those kids came from.'

'I can believe that,' said Max Ford with a wry smile. 'OK, mister . . . what did you say your name was?'

'You never asked an' I didn't say,' said Brogan.

'Well I'm askin' now,' said the sheriff.

'McNally, Brogan McNally,' replied Brogan. 'I don't go too much on the McNally bit though, Brogan is just fine. I'm a long time out of Seattle, too long to remember. I've been driftin' all my life, never been inside a prison or been arrested for any sort of crime. I pays my own way, gettin' a few dollars here an' there when I need money. I have been known to indulge in a spot of bounty huntin' an' I've even been known to work . . .' he laughed. 'That don't happen too often though, I really do have to be hard up for that to happen, an' no, I do not hire my gun out no matter how badly off I am.'

'OK, for the moment I accept what you say,' said the sheriff. 'Why this unhealthy interest in Indians? I would have thought a man like you would steer clear of trouble, particularly when you're a stranger an' don't know just how things are.'

'Try enlightenin' me, Sheriff,' suggested Brogan. 'All I know is an Indian farm was attacked by some men the Indians claim came from Cottonwood, who call themselves the Squaw Hunters. I believe the Indians when they say that those men were butchered for no other reason than Indian heads fetch five dollars apiece an' that their children were taken away to be sold. That kind of thing don't seem right to me. I ain't got no particular love for Indians or anyone else but, despite what you might believe, I don't like to see anyone treated like that.'

'Now there's somethin' you don't see very often,' sneered the sheriff. 'A saddlebum what's got morals. You heard what was said, the law allows for children like them to be sold as apprentices providin' the consent of a guardian or other responsible person is obtained. Billy Running Horse has been deemed to be their guardian; it is known that he is related to them.'

'That just sounds like legal talk for sellin' them as slaves,' said Brogan.

'Call it what you like, Mr McNally,' said the sheriff, apparently deliberately using Brogan's surname simply to annoy him. 'The fact is it is the law in this state an' there ain't a damned thing you can do about it. That applies to those Indian men as well. They are vagrants and the law states that vagrants must serve four months indentured service. If you don't like the law, Mr McNally, I suggest that you get your ass out of here, before I arrest you as a vagrant, an' go somewhere what's got different laws, laws that suit you. Do I make myself clear? The pity is that the vagrancy law only applies to Indians, blacks or mulattos an' not to white folk. Don't let that fool you, though; there are other ways I can deal with the likes of you.'

'What about these men who call themselves Squaw Hunters?' demanded Brogan. 'Does California law allow men like that to simply go round murderin' Indians, rapin' their women an' stealin' their children?'

'Them's very strong accusations,' said the sheriff.

'Maybe I can get some of the Indians to swear in court that's what happened,' said Brogan.

All three lawmen burst out laughing. 'Mr McNally,' said the sheriff, eventually. 'There's one more aspect of California law which maybe I'd better explain. The law states, quite clearly, that no Indian, black or mulatto person may give evidence either in favour of or against any white person. In other words, Mr McNally, Indians ain't allowed to accuse no white man of nothin'. Also, as far as the law is concerned, it is impossible for any white person to be accused of murderin' an Indian, black or mulatto. Nor is it against the law for anyone to call themselves just what the hell they like. Like it or not, Mr McNally, that's the law as it stands.'

'So these Squaw Hunters can kill, rape an' abduct as many Indians as they like an' get away with it an' there's not a damned thing the law can do, even if anyone wanted to.'

'That's about the size of it,' said the sheriff, with a broad grin. 'Considerin' all the men had been killed out at that farm, you sure learned a hell of a lot.'

'They missed three young men,' said Brogan. 'The one spoke very good English and claimed to have been educated by missionaries.'

'The worst kind!' said the sheriff, spitting on the floor. 'The worst thing they ever did was try to educate the Indians. What was his name?'

'I don't know, he wouldn't say,' said Brogan. 'He did say that folk like you hated educated Indians who had returned to their people.'

'Too damned right,' said the sheriff, spitting again. 'Young man you say? About twenty or somethin' like that?' He glanced at his deputies. 'That sounds like it might be Jimmy Two Rivers. Damned stupid name, but then they all have stupid names. So, Two Rivers is back, is he? He's one Indian with a price on his head. Did he say where he was goin'?'

'He said somethin' about goin' up into the hills,' said Brogan.

'Yeh, it figures,' said the sheriff. 'That young man has threatened to start a war against the white man, that's why there's a price on his head.'

'An' I reckon he's got good cause,' said Brogan.

'What you reckon don't mean a damned thing,' said the sheriff. 'That young buck is trouble.'

'What I don't understand is, if you're so dead set against the Indians, why do you use them?' said Brogan. 'I saw two Indians in uniform out on the streets last night roundin' up other Indians.'

'Indian police,' said the sheriff, with some disgust. 'Sure, we use 'em but I got to admit that my opinion of them is lower than it is for Indians like Jimmy Two Rivers. At least Two Rivers an' his kind do have somethin' they think worth fightin' for even if I don't. My private opinion of the Indian police is that they've sold out their own kind an' are lower than shit. Still, I don't have to like 'em, all I have to do is use 'em.'

Brogan shook his head, saddened by what he had heard. This was the first time he had been in California and, he decided, it was probably going to be his last. It was not that he had any great regard for Indians or blacks, but his sense of justice rebelled at the thought of people being treated differently simply because of an accident of birth. He also realized that any ideas he might have had about helping the children were simply non-starters.

'OK, Sheriff,' Brogan said. 'I guess I've learned a few things today. Am I free to go or is there some law about white saddletramps bein' at large?'

'There's been a few saddlebums who I wished I could throw in jail,' replied the sheriff. 'Sure, you're free to go. My advice still stands, get your ass outa here. It's my guess you just made yourself a few enemies by doin' what you did out there.'

'I reckon I can cope,' said Brogan. 'I'll be out of here first thing in the mornin' if that's all right with you.'

'Sooner the better,' said the sheriff.

Brogan nodded to all three lawmen and slowly ambled out into the street. The only reason he had not offered to leave Cottonwood that day was to prove to the sheriff – and to a certain extent himself – that he could not be pushed around.

As he left the sheriff's office he was suddenly surrounded by about a dozen people, all except one of them women, all congratulating him on his stand against authority.

'Now hold it!' said Brogan, raising his hands to ward off a woman who apparently wanted to kiss him. 'All I did was speak my mind. I didn't know what the law was in these parts.'

'It's a pity there aren't more men like you,' said the woman who had tried to kiss him. She suddenly sniffed hard and took a couple of steps backward as Brogan's unsavoury body odours became apparent.

'Yes, sir,' said the only man in the group, a short, plump man. 'Please allow me to shake your hand, sir.' He snatched Brogan's hand and shook it hard. 'The name's Elias Ephram Brown, most of my friends call me Eli. I'd consider it an honour if you would too. Me an' my wife . . .' he indicated the woman who had tried to kiss Brogan, 'we run a mission for down-and-out Indians and their families . . . .'

'A very worthy cause, I'm sure,' said Brogan. 'I think you folks must have got the wrong message though. It's no concern of mine what happens to Indians or anyone else. I said what I said 'cos I didn't know what the law was.'

'But you care, that's the important thing,' said Mrs Brown. 'The passion in your voice when you stood up to the minister and Mr Forgan, the auctioneer, was there for everyone to see and hear. Please, Mr . . . er. . . .' Brogan did not enlighten her. 'Please, we need men like you, men who are not afraid to stand up to authority.'

'Sorry, ma'am,' said Brogan. 'I ain't the type to settle down nor take up no particular cause other than lookin' after myself. I seen the look on your face just now when you came too close to me. The next thing you'll be doin' is suggestin' I take a bath. I'm what they call a saddlebum, ma'am, always have been an' always will be. I thank you for the offer, but in the mornin' I shall be gone from here an' pretty soon you'll forget I was ever here. I sure will.'

'So you don't really care what happens to the Indians?' asked another of the women.

'Let me put it quite simply, ma'am,' he said. 'I couldn't give an asshole what happens to them. If I think somethin's wrong I say so, that's all.'

The women all looked at each other and nodded starchily.

'It seems we have misjudged you,' said Mrs Brown. 'Come ladies, Elias, we have work to do. Good-day to you, sir.' As the ladies turned their backs on Brogan, Elias shrugged and smiled weakly and, at a sudden cough from his wife, scampered off to join them.

Brogan was aware of two men, one at each shoulder. He turned to see Sheriff Max Ford and one of his deputies. 'It would seem not everyone thinks like you do,' he said.

'The Mission of the Children of God,' said the sheriff. 'They have this notion that all men, includin' Indians, are equal in the eye of God. Maybe they'll learn one day, when an Indian rapes one of 'em.'

'Perhaps it's as well that there is someone caring for the Indians,' said Brogan.

'Oh, don't waste your sympathies on that lot,' said the sheriff. 'They run a large farm about ten miles out of town. They use Indians to do all the hard work. They don't pay 'em nothin'. They give 'em a couple of meals a day, mainly corn meal, rice an' rotten meat an' a place to get their head down an' are always surprised when the Indians say it ain't enough. I can assure you there ain't that many Indians what stay there too long on account of Mrs Brown has this thing about a good floggin' bein' the only way of drivin' the devil out of 'em. Accordin' to her all Indians are possessed by the devil. I think she just enjoys seein' 'em flogged.'

'It takes all kinds, I suppose,' said Brogan. 'I hear the saloon's open about now. I think I'll have me some of that devil's brew.'

'The best beer an' the best women are in the Cottonwood Bar,' said the sheriff. 'Mind, I ain't so sure they'll appreciate your company. O'Leary's Bar might suit you better, they don't really mind who drinks there.'

Brogan elected for the Cottonwood Bar.

THREE

The Cottonwood Bar was at the opposite end of the town to the livestock pens and, as Brogan left the sheriff's office, it appeared that the auction had been completed and quite a number of people were slowly heading in the direction of the bar.

From the reaction of almost everyone when they saw him, it seemed that Brogan had suddenly become *persona non grata*. Such a situation was not new to him and did not bother him at all. In fact it would have been unusual for him not to be *persona non grata* in most of the towns he came across. This was the lot of most saddletramps. It was noticeable that when some of the men realized that he too was heading for the Cottonwood Bar they suddenly changed their minds and either turned around or went into one of the other saloons. The majority of the women simply ignored him, or crossed the street, or turned down alleyways to avoid him.

The Cottonwood Bar was already quite full as Brogan pushed open the swing doors but all noise and action suddenly ceased as everyone turned to stare at him. For a few moments there was complete silence as Brogan crossed the floor towards the counter. Suddenly there was a shout of 'Indian-lover!' from someone, followed by other such calls and demands for him to 'Get your stinkin' ass out of here!' Brogan simply smiled and leant on the counter and ordered a beer.

'Ain't got no beer,' said the bartender.

'No beer?' queried Brogan, indicating a couple of full glasses close by. 'That sure looks like beer to me.'

'I don't think you understand, mister,' said the bartender. 'When I say I ain't got no beer that means I ain't got no beer for Indian-lovers. Now you just turn around an' get your ass out of here. I run a decent establishment an' I don't serve Indians, blacks an' mulattos 'cos it's against the law, an' I don't serve Indian-lovers on account of it ain't healthy – my health.'

Brogan glanced in the mirror behind the bar and was aware of three large men approaching. The fact that they had flipped back their jackets to reveal guns told him that they meant business. He had noticed that very few men in Cottonwood wore guns. This was not at all unusual in many towns and it was probably completely unnecessary in the normal run of things in Cottonwood. The fact that these three *were* wearing guns seemed to indicate that they had deliberately donned them hoping to pick a fight with him, or that they were employed to use guns. He did nothing, deliberately waiting for them to make the first move. He knew that the one thing they wanted was for him to act first, hoping to justify killing him.

'You heard what he said,' hissed one of the men. 'No Indians, blacks, mulattos or Indian-lovers. Now there's two ways you can leave here, mister. You either walk out of your own accord or it might just be that you get carried out in an undertaker's box. Personally I don't think you'll make as far as the door unless you can run pretty damned fast.'

'Then takin' me out in a box would be murder,' said Brogan, turning and resting one elbow on the counter. 'Maybe you can kill Indians an' get away with it, but I ain't no Indian.'

'Mister,' hissed the man again, 'you're an even lower form of life, a saddlebum *and* an Indian-lover. Bein' one or the other is bad enough, but bein' both is just about as low as any man can sink. There's maybe sixty people in this room who are witnesses to the fact that it was you who drew your gun first. I don't think you'll find even one of 'em who'd swear it was murder. I don't reckon Max Ford would bother lookin' too hard either. It's your choice, mister; dead, or try to stay alive, we don't mind which.'

'I suggest you try to put me in that box,' goaded Brogan.

'If that's the way you want it, it can be arranged,' snarled one of the other men.

Brogan casually pushed back his hat and stood up straight. The three men were obviously taken off guard by Brogan's actions and attitude and he guessed that they had expected him to turn tail and make a run for it. He was aware that running, in certain circumstances, might have been the best thing to do, but Brogan McNally had never turned tail in his life and he was too set in his ways to start now. Besides, the apparent leader of the three had more or less said that he would never make it as far as the door. His hand casually dropped to his side as he waited for one of them to make the first move. Complete silence and an air of anticipation fell upon the room but nobody stirred, the outcome was obviously a foregone conclusion. There was a sudden snarl from one of the men and all three went for their guns. . . .

There were three shots in quick succession and, as the echoes died down, Brogan was looking down on two men lying on the floor, groaning, and the third staring at blood soaking into his shirt from a wound in his arm. His gun was on the floor. There was an audible gasp from all the other customers, obviously amazed at what they had just witnessed.

'Beer!' Brogan said to the bartender as he turned. 'Beer for me an' a doctor for them.' Suddenly everyone in the bar was talking at once.

'Beer, yes, sir,' croaked the bartender, plainly not prepared to stand up to the stranger any more. He passed Brogan one of the full glasses. 'On the house, sir.'

'I can pay,' said Brogan. 'I ain't lookin' for charity.' He tossed a coin on the counter. 'Ain't anyone goin' to get the doctor?'

'No need,' said a voice. 'I'm right here.' A portly figure came forward and knelt down to examine the men on the floor. Suddenly pandemonium broke loose and almost everyone was running from the bar calling out that Carl and Steve had been killed. A few of the more curious remained out of nothing more than morbid fascination.

Brogan replaced his gun and slowly drank his beer, waiting for the inevitable arrival of Sheriff Max Ford, which was about two minutes later.

'You're under arrest, McNally!' barked the sheriff as soon as he walked in.

'On what charge, Sheriff?' asked Brogan.

The sheriff looked down at the doctor who sighed and stood up. 'They'll be OK,' he said. 'Carl has taken a bullet in the shoulder which'll have to come out an' Steve's got nothin' more than a flesh wound.' He looked at the man still standing. 'Just a scratch,' he pronounced. 'They'll all live.'

'I heard they'd all been killed,' muttered the sheriff, almost disappointed at discovering the truth. 'I'm still takin' you in, McNally,' he continued. 'For your own sake if nothin' else.'

'Do you think I need protection?' asked Brogan a little arrogantly, indicating the injured men still on the floor.

'Maybe you don't, but this town sure does,' muttered the sheriff. 'Get movin', I'll find out exactly what happened here later.' Brogan slowly and deliberately drained his beer before obeying.

There was a large crowd outside as Brogan and the sheriff left the bar. This time they were, for the most part, silent other than talking among themselves. It seemed that nobody was now prepared to call Brogan an Indian-lover or anything else after what they had just witnessed. Another reason was that Brogan was still wearing his gun.

'So what's the charge, Sheriff?' asked Brogan as he handed over his gunbelt in the sheriff's office. 'I haven't killed nobody; you heard what the doc said, just scratches.'

'Carl needs operatin' on,' said the sheriff. 'What happened?'

'It was like you said it would be,' said Brogan.

'They didn't want to serve me any beer. If it had been left to the bartender I would have just accepted it an' gone somewhere else, but before I had chance them three came on me. They said somethin' about me havin' the choice of walkin' out or bein' carried out in an undertaker's box. I think they already had the undertaker standin' by.'

'An' why didn't you just walk?'

Brogan laughed. 'I've often wondered just what it would be like to be taken out in an undertaker's box,' he said.

'An' one of these days that's just what you're goin' to find out,' muttered the sheriff. 'I said before that I wouldn't like to challenge you to a gunfight an' this just proves how right I was. Carl Edwards is faster than I am with a gun. In fact I'd say there ain't nobody in this territory who's faster. An' to take on all three of 'em sure must've been somethin' worth seein'.'

'Well, it looks like there's someone in this territory now who is faster,' said Brogan. 'If he's your best, I don't think I've got that much to worry about.'

'In a straight shoot-out, no,' said the sheriff. 'Even you wouldn't be able to do much against a bullet in the back though. Believe me, the only way most folk round here know how to fight is by shootin' in the back.'

'Mr Ford,' said Brogan with a wry smile. 'I left Seattle when I was about fourteen years old an' I've been driftin' ever since. Now I never was that good with numbers, especially when it came to countin' birthdays, but I reckon it's been gettin' on for about forty years now, maybe even a bit longer. Durin' that time I've lost count of the number of times men have tried to shoot me from almost every angle, includin' in the back. I've taken a couple of hits from time to time but I'm still here, as you can see. I reckon I've learned enough to look after myself. The day I don't will be my last an' you won't find me complainin'.'

'I'm still keepin' you here for a while,' said the sheriff. 'Right now I reckon every gun-happy kid in Cottonwood will be out lookin' to test himself against you. We've got a few young hotheads who seem to think they're faster than anyone else an' right now the last thing I need is you provin' them wrong. You told me that you'd never been inside a jail; well, here's a first. Anyhow, I want to find out exactly what happened.'

'I told you what happened,' said Brogan. 'As for never bein' inside a jail, I didn't say that. I said I'd never been in prison. There is a difference.'

'OK, so you've never been in prison,' muttered Max Ford. 'I've heard what you reckoned happened, I want to hear it from someone else.'

'Try the doc,' suggested Brogan. 'He was there. I reckon his story is as good as you're goin' to get.'

'Lock him up!' Max Ford ordered one of the deputies. 'I'm goin' out on the street. Don't let anyone near him.'

The sheriff met the doctor just outside the office and asked him if he had seen what happened.

'Max, everybody in that room saw what happened and most will remember it all their lives,' said the doc. 'One second Carl, Steve an' Hal were goin' for their guns an' the next Carl an' Steve were on the floor and Hal was clutchin' at his arm. I've never seen a man move so fast in my life. In fact I don't think anyone actually saw it happen. One second he didn't have a gun, next second he did and had used it.'

'I'm not surprised,' said the sheriff. 'There was somethin' about him which warned me somethin' like that would happen. That's not quite what I meant though. Why did Carl, Steve and Hal try to take him on?'

'Oh, that's easy,' said the doc. 'I heard Carl say he was going to kill him just on account of what he said down at the auction. It was Carl Edwards and his friends who brought those Indian kids in.'

'I figured it might be,' said the sheriff. 'OK, Doc, I think you've told me all I wanted to know.'

'Oh, there's no doubt about it, Max,' said the doc. 'Your man was acting purely in self-defence. Whether or not you agree with what he did at the auction is neither here not there. It was a fair fight as far as he was concerned, they drew first. I'm just surprised nobody was killed.'

'I agree,' said the sheriff. 'I reckon if McNally had tried to kill them there would have been three bodies on their way to the cemetery right now.'

Max Ford felt that he needed guidance as to what to do next. The doc's testimony alone meant that, as far as he was aware, he had no legal grounds on which to detain Brogan. He made his way towards the mayor's house. The mayor was also a lawyer.

On the way he was accosted several times by people demanding that the stranger be charged with something. There were also a great many not-so-veiled threats to make certain that Brogan got exactly what everyone felt he deserved. Those same people were not quite so brave when the sheriff offered to lend them his gun and stand against Brogan. However, the general mood was such that he felt an attempt would be made on Brogan's life and he was not prepared to risk even more killings.

It was not that people were looking to avenge what happened to the three men in the Cottonwood Bar; almost everyone had no feelings at all on that score. However, they completely resented anyone who showed any sympathies towards Indians. Such men were always considered troublemakers. It was, Max Ford was convinced, even more important that Brogan McNally be kept in jail either until things had calmed down or until he could be got out of town unseen.

'On the face of it there isn't a damned thing you can do but let him go,' said the mayor. 'I heard what happened and I also heard that Carl Edwards told several people that he was going to kill him. All they had to do was swear that this McNally went for his gun first. I take your point though, there are a few hotheads who just might try to do something. All I can say is that what happens to McNally isn't your problem. If he gets himself killed, so what?'

'The so what is what do I do about anyone who does kill him?' said the sheriff. 'I couldn't care less what happens to McNally. I don't think he can be killed that easy, though, an' the last thing I want is to be givin' custom to the undertaker I don't need to give. Even if McNally is killed I reckon he'll take quite a few with him.'

The mayor thought for a few moments. 'All I can suggest is that you keep him locked up until early in the morning and then make sure he leaves town. He probably won't want to stay anyway.'

'And if he insists on goin' free now?'

'Tell him you're keeping him in jail under Town Ordinance Two Six Seven.'

'Two Six Seven?' queried the sheriff. 'What the hell is Town Ordinance Two Six Seven?'

The mayor laughed. 'Actually it states that cattle, sheep, pigs, goats and other livestock shall not be allowed to wander the streets unattended and any such livestock found so doing will be corralled and that the owner shall pay a fine not exceeding ten dollars for each animal. In the event of no owner being traced, such livestock will be sold at public auction. I suppose you could classify this Brogan McNally as unattended livestock. It really doesn't matter, Max, just keep him in jail until you can get rid of him safely. I hardly think he's going to complain to any higher authority about unlawful imprisonment. Do you?'

'Town Ordinance Two Six Seven!' laughed the sheriff. 'I'll have to remember that one. I knew about animals not wanderin' the streets unattended but I never did know what law it came under. OK Sam, Two Six Seven it is.'

With the troublesome saddletramp now safely locked in jail, the town started to return to normal. There were at least three farmers leaving town, each with their new possession, an Indian child. Two of them allowed their child to ride up with them, albeit behind them, but one had tied his unfortunate child's wrists to a rope which in turn was hitched behind the wagon. The attitude seemed to be that if the child did not run fast enough to remain on its feet, it would simply be dragged along. The question of injury or even death seemed completely unimportant even though the new owner had just paid about $100 for the child.

In the office, Max Ford stared through the bars of the cell and sneered at Brogan.

'I'm keepin' you here until the mornin',' he announced. 'I cleared it with the mayor an' he's a lawyer.'

'On what charge?' queried Brogan.

'Town Ordinance Two Six Seven,' replied the sheriff, grandly.

'An' what the hell is that?' asked Brogan.

'Somethin' about public order,' said the sheriff. 'I don't know all the legal talk for it, all I need to know is that the mayor says I can hold you under it. Don't worry, I'll make sure you're out of here before first light in the mornin'. You'll be given your gun an' your horse. After that I don't ever want to see you in Cottonwood again. Do I make myself clear? Think yourself lucky, there's quite a few folk out there just itchin' to use you as target practice.'

'I've got a rifle hid in the livery,' said Brogan. 'Do I get it myself in the mornin' or will you look for it?'

'Just tell me where it is,' sighed the sheriff. 'I'll make sure it's found an' handed to you along with your horse in the mornin'. I don't want to chance nothin' goin' wrong.'

'It's underneath a pile of straw in the top right-hand corner of the stall,' said Brogan. 'A Winchester.'

'Winchester!' said the sheriff, raising his eyebrows slightly. 'No wonder you made sure it was hid. Most folk in these parts work hard all their lives an' can't afford fancy pieces like Winchesters, an' long-barrelled Colts yet here you are, a saddlebum what's never done an honest day's work in his life, with two of the finest pieces money can buy. I don't know, maybe I'm in the wrong business.'

'I ain't never done a dishonest day's work either,' reminded Brogan. 'Just make sure I get my gun, I'll be back to haunt you if I don't.'

'You'll get your gun,' muttered the sheriff. I'll go and find it myself.'

'If I have to stay here,' said Brogan. 'I want somethin' to eat. I hear tell Grace opens up her eatin' house about four o'clock.'

'You want to eat, you pay for it,' said the sheriff.

'I figured as much,' sighed Brogan. 'OK, I want a big steak, turnip greens, fried potatoes an' a large mug of coffee. I've got enough money.'

'I'm definitely in the wrong business,' muttered the sheriff. 'OK, I'll see to it. She'll be open at four.'

One of the deputies came to the door which led from the office to the cells and told his boss that four of the Indian police had arrived and that he was going out to get a breath of fresh air, muttering something about dirty saddlebums an' stinkin' Indians. Max Ford also pulled a face and shook his head and muttered something about 'scum'. He went through to the office, leaving the adjoining door ajar.

Over the years, Brogan had, amongst his other senses, developed a very keen sense of hearing. It was his boast that he could hear a fly land on a piece of dung from a distance of about 100 yards. Whilst this was an obvious exaggeration, there was no doubt that Brogan could hear things others could not and from. a greater distance than most. His ability lay not just in hearing but in being able to interpret the sounds he heard. He used his hearing ability now as he listened to what was being discussed in the other room.

'We have discovered where Jimmy Two Rivers is hiding,' said one of the Indians. 'He is with the renegades in Yellow River Valley.'

'How many of them?' asked Max Ford.

'Perhaps forty,' replied the Indian. 'They are mostly women and children. There is only Two Rivers and three or four others who will put up any resistance.'

'There's five hundred dollars out on Two Rivers,' said the sheriff. 'The likes of you an' me ain't normally allowed to collect rewards though, it's part of our job. You'll have to arrange for somebody to bring him in. It don't matter if he's alive or dead but it'll save a few awkward questions if he was brought in dead. We'll split the reward five ways.'

'What about the man we choose to bring him in?' asked one of the Indians.

'I'm quite sure you know how to deal with him,' said the sheriff.

'It is three days to the Yellow River Valley,' said one of them. 'It is also very wide and flat. It will be difficult to get close.'

'You're paid to work things like that out,' said the sheriff. 'A bunch of squaws an' kids shouldn't cause you no problem. They're your people, you should know how they'll think an' react.'

'We are not Lakota,' said one of the other Indians.

'Lakota, Pawnee, Shoshone or whatever else you care to call yourselves,' snarled the sheriff, 'you're all Indians. You just get out there an' bring me the body of Jimmy Two Rivers. I reckon you can all use a hundred dollars apiece, I know I sure can.'

About half an hour after the Indian policemen had left the office, Max Ford brought Brogan a plate of steak; turnip greens and fried potatoes. The coffee, he told Brogan, he would provide himself. Whilst Brogan was enjoying his meal, which cost him one dollar, the sheriff went off to find Brogan's Winchester and to make certain that his horse would be saddled and ready before dawn. The livery owner said that the best he was prepared to do was to saddle the horse that night so that it was ready for the morning. There was apparently no way he was prepared to get up before dawn for anyone.

Max Ford showed Brogan the rifle and told him it would be with his Colt but that both guns would be unloaded. He never did tell Brogan why.

FOUR

It was still dark when Max Ford unlocked the cell and ordered Brogan out. Brogan's guns and ammunition were on the sheriff's desk, as promised and his horse was waiting patiently outside. Brogan checked his saddle-bags and was pleasantly surprised to discover that all the supplies he had purchased were still intact. Somewhat sarcastically he thanked Max Ford for his hospitality and mounted his horse. As he did so one of the deputies appeared on horseback.

'He'll ride with you until you're well outside town limits,' said the sheriff. 'It ain't that I don't trust you – I don't. It's just to make sure nobody tries to kill you, at least not here. What happens to you after that I ain't interested in at all.'

'I appreciate your concern,' said Brogan, again sarcastically. 'I'm a big boy now though, I don't need nobody to wet-nurse me.'

'Well you've got somebody,' responded the sheriff. 'You came in from the south so I guess that means you're headed north. That's straight up past the Cottonwood Bar an' just keep on followin' your nose. Not that I need give you any advice but I will.

It's bear an' wolf country out there, big, mean bears an' wolves what'll tear you apart as soon as look at you.'

'Like I said,' said Brogan, 'I don't need nobody to wet-nurse me. I ain't never known of wolves attackin' humans yet. All the stories you hear are just that, stories. As for bears, well, I've come across plenty in my time an' I'm still here to tell the tale. I'd rather trust bears than people most of the time. At least bears don't do one thing an' mean somethin' else.'

'Yeh, you've got a point,' said the sheriff. 'Well, it's been interestin' knowin' you, McNally, if nothin' else. Just make sure I don't see your hide back in Cottonwood again or I might just skin you.'

'You could always try, I suppose,' said Brogan with a dry laugh. 'OK, deputy,' he said to his companion, 'let's go. I promise not to let any wolves or bears come too close. I don't suppose you've brought any clean underwear with you.' The implication appeared lost on the deputy but not on Sheriff Max Ford who had difficulty controlling a wry smile. As they left, four Indian policemen appeared, obviously kitted out for a few days out in the hills; their target, Yellow River Valley and Jimmy Two Rivers. Max Ford held them back until Brogan and the deputy had left.

The two men rode in almost complete silence for more than twenty minutes, the deputy not responding to any of Brogan's initial questions or comments. It was not until Brogan casually mentioned the Indian police that there was any reaction at all from the deputy.

'Scum!' he muttered. spitting on the ground. 'Slit

your throat as soon as look at you. Still, I suppose they have their uses.'

'Like trackin' down this Jimmy Two Rivers?' prompted Brogan.

'Somethin' like that,' the deputy muttered again. 'They're good trackers, I'll give 'em that.'

'I heard that Two Rivers is up in some place called Yellow River Valley,' said Brogan. 'Where's that?'

'What you want to know for?' demanded the deputy, suspiciously.

'I just want to avoid the place,' said Brogan. 'It strikes me a place like that ain't such a healthy place for a white man to be right now.'

'Well it won't cause you no problems,' responded the deputy. 'You're headin' north an' Yellow River Valley is north-east of Cottonwood, two or three days' ride. I ain't too sure, I ain't never been there. Maybe it's as well it ain't this direction. Them four Indians were goin' up there an' I wouldn't like to trust 'em.'

'That's all right then,' said Brogan. 'I guessed that was where they were goin'.' Once again silence descended on the pair for a while.

The first rays of the morning sun were just beginning to filter through the trees when Brogan suddenly brought his horse to a halt and stared ahead and listened intently.

'What you stopped for?' demanded the deputy.

'We've got company,' said Brogan.

'Company!' said the deputy. 'What company?'

'Bear type company,' said Brogan, grinning. 'About twenty yards ahead.' Immediately the deputy had grabbed his rifle and was peering wide-eyed through the trees. 'Grizzly too, I'd say,' continued

Brogan. 'They're the worst kind. Very unpredictable, grizzlies are.' The deputy was now looking about obviously very alarmed.

'How the hell do you know all that?' he demanded. 'You're just tryin' to spook me. There ain't no grizzly nor any other kind of bear up there. If there was you'd've gone for your gun.'

'Son,' said Brogan. 'Pistols are no use at all against most bears an' especially grizzlies. Even with a rifle you'd need a darned good shot or a bloody lucky one to stop a fully grown grizzly.' The deputy looked round fearfully and then at Brogan's laughing face.

'I don't know what your game is, McNally,' he said, 'but I know you're just tryin' to scare me. Well it won't work. I was told to escort you as far as Hog Back Ridge an' that's where I'm takin' you.'

'Oh, I ain't tryin' to scare you, Deputy,' said Brogan with a laugh. 'You're doin' a pretty good job of that all by yourself. There's a bear up there all right. You just keep on ridin' an' you'll soon find out. I'd say he probably made a kill or found somebody else's kill. Wolves you can scare away from a meal but bears, especially grizzlies, don't take kindly to be bein' disturbed. I reckon we ought to wait here for a while until he's finished eatin'.'

The deputy was plainly uncertain as to what to do next. 'There ain't no way you could know what's up there,' he eventually said. 'I didn't see or hear nothin'.'

'That's 'cos you, like most folk, don't know how to listen or look,' said Brogan. 'To be fair though, it ain't somethin' that can be taught very easily. It comes with years of practice. You hear somethin' an it's probably just a noise. I hear somethin' an' I can usually tell you what made that noise. It's the same with seein' things. Some birds fly into the air an' you don't think about why. Maybe it's you what's scared 'em, maybe it ain't. It's the knowin' when it ain't you that can save your life sometimes. In this case I heard a bear growl, probably warnin' some wolves off. I've heard it many times before.'

'Bullshit!' said the deputy. 'Nobody can tell so much from one bear growlin', if it was a bear.'

'Not even your Indian trackers?' asked Brogan.

'They're closer to animals than humans,' grunted the deputy.

'Tell you what,' said Brogan. 'Why don't we get off our horses an' climb to the top of that rock . . .' He indicated a large rock among the trees. 'I reckon you'll be able to see him from there.'

'Yeh . . . well . . . OK,' agreed the deputy, dismounting. Brogan, too, dismounted but on this occasion he did take his rifle with him. They led their horses away from the trail and as close to the rock as they could.

From the top of the rock they could, as Brogan had predicted, look down on the trail. Again, as Brogan had said there would be, they saw a large bear in the process of tearing at a deer carcass.

'Yep, it's grizzly,' said Brogan with a certain smug satisfaction.

'Well, I'll be . . .' muttered the deputy. 'How in the name of hell did you know he was there? I never heard nothin' an' I sure as hell never saw nothin'. What do we do now?'

'We wait,' said Brogan. 'We wait like them wolves have to wait.' He pointed at some trees behind the bear. 'They won't be no bother. We just ride straight through 'em. They'll be interested in that carcass, not in us.'

'Hell!' muttered the deputy. 'You just ain't human. You sure you ain't no kin to a bear?'

'Bears might be big an' fierce but at least they is predictable,' said Brogan. 'I ain't found many humans what is predictable.'

They waited for about ten minutes before Brogan nudged the deputy and told him it was time to go. The deputy was plainly not quite so certain and checked, for at least the tenth time, that his rifle was loaded.

They rejoined the trail where Brogan listened intently for a while before nodding that it was safe to proceed. The deputy was still not quite convinced and remained behind Brogan.

By the time they reached the deer carcass, the bear was slowly ambling up a slope, grumbling to himself, and the wolves were beginning to close in. On seeing the two humans the wolves drew back, baring their teeth and snarling. The bear stopped briefly and looked back. He gave a loud roar but then continued up the slope to disappear amongst the trees. The deputy was plainly rather more concerned about the wolves and was about to shoot one of them when Brogan stopped him.

'Just keep on ridin',' he commanded. 'They'll back off.'

The deputy lowered his rifle and kept on riding even though his horse was obviously terrified. Brogan's horse, on the other hand, was an old-timer at such things and more or less ignored the wolves. The deputy breathed a big sigh of relief when the wolves ignored him and closed in on the carcass.

'Man!' he croaked, pulling alongside Brogan. 'I ain't never been so scared in my life. It didn't twig with me before, but I see what you mean about clean underwear.'

'I'd've thought you'd be used to bears an' wolves,' said Brogan.

'Mister,' said the deputy. 'My home town is San Francisco. San Francisco is a big city right next to the ocean. I don't suppose you know what the ocean looks like. Well it's water as far as . . .'

'I was born an' raised in Seattle,' said Brogan. 'That's right on the coast too. I left on account of I didn't fancy goin' to sea to work an' to get away from the stink of fish an' whale meat.'

'Is there nothin' you don't know or somewhere you haven't been?' demanded the deputy.

'I ain't never been to San Francisco,' said Brogan with a wry smile.

'OK, I guess I asked for that,' said the deputy. 'Well, I've only been in Cottonwood for six months. I left San Francisco for pretty much the same reasons you left Seattle. Durin' that time I've only ever seen two bears, both of them from a safe distance an' I ain't never been that close to a pack of wolves before. I got pretty close to a lone wolf once but that's all.'

'Then just remember that wolves won't attack humans,' said Brogan. 'Sometimes they might be interested in his horse but I'll guarantee they won't touch a live human. I have heard of 'em eatin' corpses but I doubt even that. I reckon human meat makes 'em sick. Whatever it is, all the stories you've heard about wolves attackin' a man just ain't true.'

'What about bears?' asked the deputy.

'Bears is different,' said Brogan. 'Sometimes they'll just walk straight past you like you don't even exist. Sometimes they'll just suddenly charge at you out of the trees for no other reason than they're in a bad temper. The thing is never to annoy 'em, especially when they're feedin'. Another thing is never to place yourself between a bear an' open country or a forest. The worst thing you could ever do is get between a mother bear an' her cub. I'll guarantee you'll never be able to stop her. In other words if you come across one what ain't got no way of escape, you get the hell out of there before he charges. I've seen bears that've had more'n a dozen rounds pumped into them, even in their head an' they still keep on comin'. For the most part though, if you leave them alone they'll leave you alone.'

'Thanks for the advice,' said the deputy. 'Hog Back Ridge is about a mile up the road. What'll you do now?'

'Just keep on movin',' said Brogan.

'Are you headin' for anywhere in particular?'

'I guess we're all headin' somewhere,' said Brogan. 'I suppose I'm always lookin', always dreamin'. I ain't never found what I'm lookin' for yet an' I guess I'm too old to expect to find it now.'

'That don't seem much of a life to me,' said the deputy.

'I guess it ain't for most,' admitted Brogan. 'It's my kind of life though. I think I'd rather be mauled to death by a grizzly than end up dyin' in some bed after spendin' a life workin' for other folk. This way I go where an' when I please, even sleep all day if I want to. I've got no woman to nag at me an' make me get into a tub of water just to make me smell pretty.'

'Don't you miss havin' a woman?'

'What's to miss? I get my share now an' then. Do you have a woman?'

'I'm courtin' Mary, the sheriff's daughter,' said the deputy. 'She's all for gettin' wed as soon as possible but I ain't so sure.'

'Love 'em an' leave 'em, as they say,' said Brogan.

'Mary ain't like that,' sighed the deputy. 'No marriage, no lovin' she says. I guess she's right. I'd just like to try before I buy though. I'm twenty-three an' I'm ashamed to say I ain't never been with a woman.'

'That ain't nothin' to be ashamed of. If it's botherin' you then find yourself a whore,' advised Brogan. 'A good whore will teach you all you need to know.'

'In Cottonwood!' exclaimed the deputy. 'Hell, somethin' like that'd be all round the town before I'd finished with her. That'd be it as far as Mary is concerned. She an' her Aunt Martha run some sort of society what's tryin' to rid the town of all whorehouses and prostitutes. I don't think they'll get very far though. Why she even feels sorry for the Indian kids sold into apprenticeships.'

'And that's bad?' queried Brogan.

'Feelin' sorry for Indians?' said the deputy with a laugh. 'Hell, what's there to feel sorry for?' Brogan let the subject drop but until that point he had almost forgotten about the plight of the Indians. The subject now began to occupy his thoughts once again. They rode on in silence for another ten minutes when the deputy stopped.

'Hog Back Ridge,' said the deputy pointing at a long, low ridge. 'This is as far as I go.'

'Just remember what I said about wolves an' bears,' said Brogan. 'You leave them alone an' for the most part they'll leave you alone. Don't waste bullets on bears, just run like hell if they come at you.'

'I'll remember,' promised the deputy. 'Good luck, Mr McNally.'

'You too, Deputy,' said Brogan.

Brogan watched the deputy disappear from view, all the time wondering about Jimmy Two Rivers and the Indian children. There was nothing he could do to help those children who were now the property of farmers or traders, he knew that, but that did nothing to quell his sense of injustice. The plight of Jimmy Two Rivers on the other hand was something else.

The Indian police had apparently been dispatched to find Two Rivers and take his dead body back to Cottonwood. That apart, Brogan had the feeling that the Indian women in the valley would almost certainly be slaughtered. The children might just escape slaughter and end up being sold. The plight of Jimmy Two Rivers suddenly took second place to the plight of the women and children.

The deputy had told him that Yellow River Valley was north-east of Cottonwood, which meant that if he were to strike off in a north-easterly direction he would eventually reach the valley. At times like this Brogan had a habit of talking to his horse and this was no exception.

'OK, old girl,' he said. 'You decide. Carry on

north an' forget all about 'em or head north-east?' His horse shook her head. 'Now what in the name of hell does that mean?' he asked. 'No, we don't head north or no, we don't head north-east? OK, I'll make it easy for you. Do we head north-east an' try to help them Indians?' The horse shook her head. 'Your trouble is you're gettin' old,' muttered Brogan. 'There was a time when you was only too ready for some action. Is that your last word?' This time she nodded her head. Brogan was quite convinced that his horse understood every word he said. 'One of these days I'm goin' to get round to givin' you a name,' he said. 'OK, I asked you what you wanted to do, but I'm in charge here and I say we head off north-east to this Yellow River Valley. This time you've got to move a mite faster'n you usually do as well, I want to get there before them Indian police if I can.'

There had never been any question, as far as he was concerned, as to what he was going to do. It had simply become a habit of his to talk to his horse whenever a decision had to be made. Although he rarely took the animal's apparent advice, he felt that she was wiser than he was at times.

There was no obvious easy route to the north-east. The mountainsides were thickly wooded and steep which would have made for hard, slow going. There was a river running out of the mountains, down a valley which lay in a generally north-easterly direction, but a very short excursion along the river into the valley soon convinced him that it would be almost impossible to get through. The river was full of rocks, raging water and cut through sheer, thirty-foot sides. The only way appeared to be along the top of Hog Back Ridge, and even that, although largely devoid of trees, did not look too easy. However, there was little alternative. An hour later, on looking back from the top of the ridge, he could still see the trail and the point where he had parted company with the deputy.

As he looked back, a sudden flight of birds further back along the trail made him stop and wait. His wait of about five minutes was not in vain; five riders appeared, one of them with his arm in a sling. Even from where he was, on Hog Back Ridge, and at least a mile away, Brogan recognized Carl Edwards and two of the other men. He was very surprised that Edwards was up and about so soon after his injury and operation to remove the bullet.

Now what the hell brings you out here this early in the mornin'? he asked himself. Somehow I don't think you're out just to exercise your horses. He saw them stop and examine the ground, one of them pointing along the river. Another pointed in the direction of Hog Back Ridge, apparently directly at Brogan, but he did not give the impression of having seen Brogan. The men turned off the trail and headed for the ridge. There was now no doubting just what – or who – their objective was.

Brogan urged his horse to greater speed; she seemed to appreciate the need and co-operated. It took the better part of an hour to reach the end of Hog Back Ridge. From then on his route was determined for him along a deer track by the rise of an almost sheer mountainside to his left and another almost sheer drop down to a rapidly flowing, rock-strewn river about 200 feet below. He assumed this was the same river he had thought about negotiating before. As he joined the deer track, he looked back along the ridge but there was no sign of the five men he assumed were following him. However, he did not doubt that they were still on his tail. The deer track was slightly easier going and he urged his horse a little faster.

It must have been over two hours later before deer track and river slowly came together. From that point onwards the going along the river was easier. The valley rose quite sharply but also widened out, eventually coming out on to a large, flat, marshy area. Despite its being flat, the ground became softer and slowed down his progress quite considerably. However, it did not bother him, he knew that it was the same for the men following, although there was still no sign of them.

The marshy ground eventually gave way to drier, coarse-grassed, rolling hillsides and the wind suddenly turned very cold. Had it not been for the men following him, Brogan might well have elected to make camp alongside one of the many small, clear streams which crossed the area, and to make a fire. However, since it was still about three or four hours until sunset, he decided to keep going and hope to find somewhere where he could camp unseen.

About two hours later, much to his surprise, he came across sheep and a rough, stone-built cabin. It was obviously occupied although the occupants did not come out to greet him. A dark, heavily lined face appearing briefly at a window told him that these particular sheep farmers were also Indians. It seemed that, unlike other Indians he had come across, the Indians of California had adopted the white man's life style. However, like all other Indians he had come across since he had been in California, they seemed frightened of any white man. Having seen and heard what he had, he did not blame them. He decided to keep on riding and not disturb them. As he drew away, he saw four figures appear. One of them was obviously a man and the other three were women, two of them apparently quite young.

About half a mile from the Indians' cabin he came across the remains of another stone cabin alongside a clear stream. He decided that this was an ideal place to rest up for the night. It was well placed to be defended if necessary.

He lit a fire and started to cook himself a simple meal of beans and dried meat. It was while he was stirring his pot that the thought of what might happen to the Indians he had seen in the cabin occurred to him. There were two young women; two young women who might just prove irresistible to squaw hunters.

FIVE

Suddenly Brogan's hunger disappeared and he laid his pot to one side. He took up his rifle and checked that it was fully loaded. There was no real need for him to check, it was nothing more than a precautionary habit. He also checked his Colt, again out of nothing more than habit.

'You just stay here, old girl,' he said to his horse. 'I reckon there's a bit of business what needs my attention. I shouldn't be too long.' The horse appeared completely indifferent, having found some tasty grass.

He eventually came within sight of the Indians' cabin but could not get closer than about 100 yards without the risk of being seen and the last thing he wanted was to frighten the occupants. As yet there was no sign of the five men following him but he sensed that they would appear very soon.

Activity around the cabin seemed to be quite normal; two of the women were obviously preparing food and the third wielding an axe to chop wood. The man sat on a small barrel smoking, leaving all the work to the women, a practice common amongst all Indian tribes. The young woman chopping wood saw the approaching men before Brogan did and suddenly they all disappeared inside the cabin.

Carl Edwards called out as he and his men approached the cabin and it was obvious that there was no reply. The men laughed and talked among themselves for a short time and eventually two of them dismounted and immediately kicked in the door of the cabin. Brogan held his fire, waiting to see what happened next.

There was a shout and cry from inside and one of the men reappeared dragging one of the two young women behind him.

'Look at what I've found,' he called, laughing loudly. 'I reckon this is as good a place as any to spend the night, we've got all the comforts of home, fresh-cooked food an' women.'

The other man appeared, pushing the Indian man in front of him and they were closely followed by the two other women. By this time all the men were off their horses, Carl Edwards checking what was in the pot the women had been preparing and two of the men leering at the other young woman who recoiled in horror. The old woman placed herself between her daughter and the men in a misguided and vain attempt to protect her daughter.

'A lone white man!' Edwards suddenly snapped at the Indian man. 'A lone white man must have come this way not that long ago. Did you see him?' The old man nodded. 'How long ago? Which way did he go?' The old man mumbled a reply but Brogan was unable to hear what he said, so, apparently, was Edwards. 'Speak up, old man!' shouted Edwards. 'I can't hear you.' To reinforce his order he slapped the old man about the face, knocking him to the ground.

'He passed by about an hour ago,' interrupted the young woman who had been dragged from the cabin, speaking almost perfect English. 'He did not stop, he just kept on riding.' She helped the old man to his feet and glared at Edwards.

Edwards looked up at the sky and grunted. 'He'll probably be camped up somewhere now. He ain't too far ahead; I reckon if we make an early start we should catch him up. OK, we stay here for the night.' He leered at the young woman. 'Like my friend said, we've got all the comforts of home right here.'

'You are welcome to share our food,' the young woman said, backing away a few paces. 'It is not much but you are welcome to what we have.'

'You can bet your life we're goin' to have your food,' snarled Edwards.

'That ain't all we're goin' to share,' sneered one of the men, making a grab at her. 'Quite the pretty one, ain't you? It must get lonely for you up here with only an old man like him for comfort. Old men like him ain't no good to any woman, we'll show you what a real man is like.'

'He is my father!' said the woman, pulling herself away from his grasp.

'All the more reason for you to appreciate it when a real man does come along then,' said the man, laughing and grabbing at her again.

'The food!' she cried, again struggling but this time failing to release herself. 'It must be cooked.'

'The old hag can see to that,' grated the man. 'While it's cookin' you an' me is goin' to . . .'

The shot echoed around the sides of the valley and the man never did complete his sentence. The other two women screamed in terror and ran inside the cabin as the man fell, remarkably slowly, to the ground, his fingers clutching at the young woman's skirts and almost pulling them off. Even Brogan, from where he was, could see blood streaming from the side of his head.

Actually, Brogan cursed. He had aimed the shot at the man's shoulder but at the vital moment the man had stumbled and lowered his head slightly. Brogan consoled himself with the thought that he had been lucky to hit the man from a distance of about 100 yards. The young woman and the old man rushed into the cabin, slammed the door and the sound of a bar being placed across it could be heard.

The other four had immediately raced for what cover there was and for a few moments there was silence. Eventually Carl Edwards called out.

'McNally! Is that you, McNally?'

'No, I'm his ghost,' called Brogan. 'Sorry about your friend, I didn't mean to kill him. It must be I'm gettin' a little rusty. I guess he ain't no real loss to nobody though. Why are you followin' me?'

'How'd you know we was followin' you?' demanded Edwards.

'You sure didn't make no effort to hide the fact,' said Brogan. 'I had you sighted from the moment you cut along the Hog Back. Besides, you just asked those folk if I'd passed by.'

'I want you, McNally,' snarled Edwards. 'I aim to kill you. No man does what you did to me an' lives to tell the tale. You made a mistake then, McNally, an' you just made another, even bigger mistake now. You just murdered a white man. That makes you an outlaw an' all outlaws, especially saddletramps, is fair game.'

'It wasn't murder,' said Brogan. 'I was protectin' an innocent woman from bein' raped. I reckon even California has laws about rapin' women.'

'She's Indian,' replied Edwards with a scornful laugh. 'There ain't no law about rapin' Indian women. That makes it murder.'

Brogan had the nasty feeling that Edwards was probably right and that in the eyes of the law as it stood in California he *was* now guilty of murder. Even so he did not believe it to be murder despite what the law might say, if it ever came to that. However, he realized that he had probably created another problem for himself and that it would be most unwise to attempt to prove his point in court, especially a Californian court. Common sense told Brogan that he had to leave the jurisdiction of Californian law as soon as possible, which would also mean abandoning these Indians and Jimmy Two Rivers. Nevertheless, as far as he was concerned, there was no question as to what he had to do next, he simply could not ride away and forget them. That was not his nature.

'I'll take my chance with the law,' called Brogan. 'Right now the only law is me an' my gun. Care to argue the point?'

'If that's the way you want it, that's fine by me,' called Edwards.

Suddenly several shots hit the ground well short of where Brogan was and he was quite happy for them to waste their bullets, knowing that he was well beyond the range of their pistols. They did have rifles but in their haste to get at the women, they had left these on their horses and there was no way, at that moment, that they could get to them. After the first volley of shots the men too realized that Brogan was out of range.

'OK, you've got the upper hand for the moment but it won't last,' called Edwards. 'What you just did to Zac is a hangin' offence but I aim to make sure you don't live to see the end of a rope, even though I'd get almost as much pleasure from seeing your legs kickin' about while your neck was stretchin'.'

'I don't intend to see the end of a rope either,' called Brogan. 'The only difference is I intend to live. Now, unless you all want to taste lead, get the hell out of here right now. Go back the way you came, that way you might just live to tell Max Ford what happened and why.' To reinforce his instruction, Brogan fired a shot close to Carl Edwards, whom he could just see behind a water butt.

'Go shit, McNally!' called Edwards. 'The only way you'll get us off your back is to kill us all.'

'That's easy to arrange if that's the way you want it,' replied Brogan, firing another shot, this time hitting the water butt. Water immediately started to gush out. 'That's the last warnin',' he continued. 'Next time you'll end up like your friend Zac, a hole in your head.' There was a somewhat hasty exchange of words between the men and for a few minutes everything went quiet.

'Have you ever seen Indians roasted alive?' called Edwards. A flaming clump of dry grass was suddenly hurled on to the thatched roof of the cabin and it took hold very quickly. 'They've got a choice, McNally,' Edwards called again. 'They can stay inside an' die or they can try to make a run for it.'

'Why them?' called Brogan. 'Your quarrel is with me.'

'Sure it is,' called Edwards. 'I just figured that since you're an Indian-lover you wouldn't be able to stand by an' watch 'em bein' slaughtered. I'll give 'em a couple of minutes an' then they'll be out.'

The thatch was now well alight and creating a lot of smoke, smoke which slowly drifted between the cabin and their horses making it very difficult to see anything. One of the men suddenly took advantage of the smoke and ran towards the horses. Brogan did shoot but it appeared that his shot missed. He could just about make out the man collecting their rifles. Again, using the smoke as cover, he ran back to the cabin and tossed a rifle to each man.

'I guess that evens things up a bit,' called Edwards. 'OK, McNally, it's your move. Let's see just how good you really are.'

There was still no sign of the Indians and no way that Brogan could get any closer without presenting Edwards and his men with an easy target. However, nature suddenly played into Brogan's hands as the wind died down and the smoke enveloped both cabin and the men. He could hear them coughing but they did not attempt to get away from the smoke. Brogan did not need to think about what to do next.

Out of nothing more than pure instinct, Brogan found himself racing across the open space and throwing himself behind another rock bringing him to within about twenty yards of the cabin. Miraculously it appeared that he had not been seen.

The wind picked up again and cleared the smoke.

This time he was able to see all four men and was just about to take aim on Edwards when the door of the cabin opened and the four Indians ran out, coughing and spluttering, the old man placing himself between Brogan and his target.

Get your ass out of it! Brogan snarled to himself. One of the young women pulled her father away but by that time Edwards had moved. It seemed that they still thought Brogan was in his original position. One of the men appeared and grabbed the old man and the woman, but Brogan was unable to draw a clear line on him. Another of the men grabbed the other young woman. This time Brogan was able to see him clearly and fired.

The shot obviously hit the man but apparently caused nothing more serious than a scratch. However, it was enough to make him release the woman. At the same time the other young woman dragged her father away.

Brogan's second shot was taken in haste and missed its target just as the Indians suddenly ran clear of the cabin. Brogan fired another shot as one of the men took aim on the fleeing Indians. The shot apparently hit the man's hand as he gave a cry of pain and dropped the rifle.

'Very clever, McNally,' called Edwards.

'Not clever enough,' called Brogan. 'Two of you should've been dead. OK, Edwards, the next move is up to you. I like the odds much better now. Three cripples, you an' the two I've just winged an' one otherwise healthy man who couldn't hit a barn from ten paces. You can either stop an' fight it out or you can get the hell out of here. I don't want to have to kill you. The choice is yours though.'

'You're prepared to let us go?' queried one of the men.

'That's what I said,' confirmed Brogan.

The four could be heard talking amongst themselves for a few moments before one of them spoke. 'It looks like we ain't got much choice,' the man called. 'OK, we're pullin' back, don't shoot.'

'That *would* be murder,' called Brogan. 'I told Max Ford an' I'm tellin' you, I don't commit murder. Don't worry, I won't shoot. Just get your butts out of here an' don't let me see you again. Next time I won't be so accommodatin'. Oh, an' one more thing. If I so much as hear one whisper that you did anythin' to these people, I'll make it my business to hunt you down. You got that?'

'I hear you, McNally,' called Edwards. 'You just remember this. Nobody gives a shit what happens to Indians. From now on you're a marked man. If the law don't get you then I will.'

'I'll take my chance with both you an' the law,' said Brogan. 'Now move before I change my mind. There's a bullet aimed straight at your head an' bullets don't care which side of the law they're on.'

The four men slowly stood up and peered in Brogan's direction, but he was well hidden from view behind the rock. Two of them picked up Zac's body and bundled it across his horse and eventually they all retreated in the direction they had come. Brogan waited until they were well away before slowly approaching the cabin. The danger might have passed for the moment but he was quite certain that he had not seen the last of Carl Edwards.

'It's OK,' he called out to the Indians who were about 100 yards up the hillside. 'You can come back,

I don't mean you no harm.' For a few moments they did not move and it was only when Brogan called out again that they slowly returned. Eventually they were standing in a line, looking suspiciously at Brogan and with a certain amount of despair at their burning cabin. The young Indian woman who spoke English slowly came towards him.

'It would have been better for you to let them have their way with us,' she said. 'We know those men, they are what the people of Cottonwood call squaw hunters. You have just placed yourself in great danger.'

'Maybe so,' nodded Brogan as the others slowly came forward. 'I ain't no squaw hunter though. I couldn't stand by an' watch. They probably would have killed you.'

'You are a white man,' said the old man. 'White men do not care what happens to Indians.'

'Well this is one white man what does care,' replied Brogan. 'The fact that you happen to be Indians don't mean nothin' to me. I'd be doin' the same if you were white, black, yellow or any other colour. They've gone for now but I have the feelin' that they'll be back. I can't stay here to protect you.'

'Then you must leave,' said the old man. 'Do not worry about us. We will take to the hills until the danger is gone. We have had to do such a thing before.'

'Then I'd get the hell out of here right now,' advised Brogan. 'They've pulled back but it won't be long before they return an' if they find you here I reckon they'll kill you all. You've got about an hour until nightfall.'

'You are right, we must leave now,' said the young

woman. 'You too must leave, it is you they really want.'

'Don't you worry none about me,' said Brogan. 'I've had men like them out to kill me more times than I can count an' I'm still here. There's just one thing. I'm a stranger in these parts an' I'm lookin' for somebody. I have to warn him that the Indian police are out to kill him. I'm headed for a place called Yellow River Valley. Do you know where it is?'

'Then the man you seek must be the one known as Jimmy Two Rivers,' replied the old man. 'I have heard that he has returned. To find Yellow River Valley the easiest way is to first find the Yellow River . . .'

'That'd be fine if I knew which river that was,' said Brogan.

'Then keep on riding in the direction you now ride,' said the old man. 'From here the Yellow River is about half a day's ride. There are other, smaller rivers between here and the Yellow River but you will know when you have reached it. It is much wider and deeper than the others and certain times of the year it assumes the colour of yellow, which is why it is called the Yellow River.'

'That makes sense I suppose,' said Brogan. 'What colour is it right now?'

'It is not yellow,' said the old man, 'but you will still know when you reach it. From there you keep on following the river upstream and you will reach Yellow River Valley.'

'How long an' have you any idea where Two Rivers might be?'

'Another half-day,' said the old man. 'Those of my

people who are there could be anywhere. They move their village regularly to avoid the white man. They are known as renegades and are outside the white man's law.'

'Seems to me all Indians are outside the white man's law,' said Brogan.

'You are right,' said the young woman. 'But there is little we can do. Now, we must leave for the hills. There are some caves we sometimes use. We will be safe there. I worry about you though.'

'Like I said,' said Brogan, 'don't you worry none about me. I've been in worse situations. Are you sure you'll be all right?'

'Yes,' she assured. 'We have used the caves many times before. If we are not here when those men return there will be no danger.' She looked sadly at the burning building. 'Everything we owned was in there, but there was little inside of any great importance.' She spoke to the other two women who immediately started to gather what few possessions they had which had not been touched by the fire. 'Our sheep will be safe enough. We shall rebuild our cabin and gather them when it is safe to do so.'

'You speak very good English,' said Brogan.

'I was taught by the same missionaries who taught Jimmy Two Rivers,' she said. 'I am pleased he has returned. Like him, I have returned to my people. I was promised to him in marriage.'

'Then I hope he comes through,' said Brogan.

He waited until the family had gathered what belongings they could carry which, in the absence of a horse or mule was not all that much. Then, as they trekked towards the hills, he returned to his horse.

'We're movin' on, old girl,' he said to his horse.

'I've decided this place is too open. We'll find somewhere up among the rocks.'

The meal he had been preparing was now cold, congealed and alive with flies but he decided that it would be a shame to waste it and proceeded to eat it cold after wafting away the flies. He had eaten worse and it was one of his rules never to waste food. That was a rule developed very early on in his career on the basis that it might be several days before he ate again, although he was now an expert at finding food where none seemed to exist.

He moved on and eventually, just as darkness was closing in, he discovered a small cave which looked back along the valley; an ideal place from which to look and listen for approaching riders.

'I say we get back an' tell the sheriff what happened,' said one of the men with Carl Edwards. 'We've got to get Zac's body back anyhow. I could do with the doc lookin' at my hand too.'

Carl Edwards looked at his companion's hand and sneered. 'That's nothin'! I say we keep on goin' after McNally,' he snarled. 'We bury Zac here. He ain't got no family so it don't matter where the hell he's buried an' the only churches he's ever been in in his life was to rob 'em. If there is such places as heaven an' hell then I know where he's gone.'

'Before he put that bullet in your shoulder I'd've said you were a match for any man,' said Steve, one of the men also injured in the Cottonwood Bar. 'Even without that, havin' seen the way he handled himself I'd say you've eventually met a man what's a whole lot faster'n you or anyone else I've ever seen. If he'd really wanted to he could have picked us all off one by one back there.'

'Yeh!' grunted Edwards. 'He's damned good, I'll give him that. More fool him for not killin' us while he had the chance. I still say we go after him. We just have to make sure he don't have the chance to draw on us. Don't you go frettin' about me, I can still use a gun. It's my left shoulder what's been shot up, not my shootin' arm.' To accentuate the point he drew his pistol and aimed it at one of the men.

'OK,' said the man, pushing the gun to one side. 'So you can still use a gun. I've been thinkin'. I don't know if he knows it or not,' he continued, 'but the way he's goin' will more'n like take him up into Yellow River Valley. Didn't you say somethin' about them Indian police bein' sent up there after that Jimmy Two Rivers?'

'So what?' asked Edwards.

'So, we get them to go after McNally,' he replied. 'They go after McNally an' if there's any shootin' it's more'n like it'll be them what gets killed if they don't manage to kill him. Killin' Indian police will put him right outside the law.'

'I want him myself,' grunted Edwards. 'I don't want no Indians takin' credit for killin' him.'

'So let them go after him,' said the man. 'We tell 'em there's been a bounty posted for him – alive. They take him, we take the Indians and McNally and claim it was him who killed the Indians.'

'If they don't kill him first,' muttered Edwards.

'Which is why I said tell 'em there's a bounty out on him alive,' stressed the man. 'You know as well as I do those bastards will do anythin' to make a few dollars.'

'I think it's a good idea,' said Steve. 'We know just

how handy McNally is with a gun; they don't, an' if we tell 'em there's about a thousand dollars' reward I know they won't be able to resist it. We let them do all the hard work of followin' him, we just follow them.'

'OK, I'll go along with that,' Edwards agreed. 'In the meantime I'm all for goin' back to that cabin. The fire will have burned itself out by now I reckon but at least the walls will still be standin' an' it'll be somewhere to shelter. It's more'n like that McNally has moved on. I didn't see his horse anywhere.'

'I reckon the Indians will have taken to the hills,' said Steve.

'I don't give a shit where they've gone,' muttered Edwards. 'There might even be some food still there. Anyhow, we ain't got no spade to dig a grave with. We'll take Zac back there. There's sure to be somethin' we can use to dig a grave with.'

'Food ain't no problem,' said Steve. 'There was a whole load of sheep round that cabin.'

'I hate mutton!' Edwards complained.

'Mutton is better'n nothin',' Steve pointed out.

'I guess so,' grumbled Edwards.

SIX

Brogan spent a peaceful night in the cave and had lit a fire, reasonably certain that Carl Edwards would not make any attempt to follow him that night. However, he was still convinced that Edwards was not a man to give up so easily and as the first rays of light broke over the mountains, he was on his way.

The old man's prediction of the Yellow River being about another half-day's ride proved to be very accurate. There had been several other rivers which he had been forced to cross and he was quite convinced that none of them was the Yellow River since they were neither very wide nor very deep.

Brogan looked up at the sun and calculated that it was exactly midday when he came upon a fairly wide, obviously quite deep river. As was the way of things, it seemed to Brogan that the easier going was on the opposite bank. However, the thought of immersing his body in water coupled with the fact that due to his almost pathological dislike of water he had never learned to swim, persuaded him to make the best of his situation and follow the bank he was on.

At various vantage-points he looked back, knowing that Edwards was probably not too far behind, but there was no sign of him. Actually, he was not only on the look-out for Edwards and his men, he was also on the look-out for the four Indian policemen who had been sent to find Jimmy Two Rivers.

How these Indian policemen would react if he did come across them he had no idea, but he suspected that the encounter would not be too friendly. At that point he also had no idea whether the Indians were in front of or behind him. Whether in front or behind, he knew that he could not treat them with quite the same disdain or contempt that he felt for Edwards and his men. These were Indians, Indians who probably knew the territory very well and were, by their very birth and nature, quite a different proposition in these conditions from the four white men.

In the towns and cities, particularly in California it seemed to him, the Indian was a most pathetic sight. It also struck him that the Californian Indian was an even more miserable sight than elsewhere. It appeared that here more so than anywhere else he had been, their traditional way of life had been almost completely destroyed and, in an attempt to survive, they had adopted many of the ways of their white masters. From what he had seen so far the adoption of the white man's ways had not been very successful. All this however, did not lessen his regard for the Indian as a tracker and as a master of the wilderness.

The old man had said that Yellow River Valley was about another half-day's ride once he found the Yellow River, but as nightfall approached it was apparent that he still had some distance to go before he found the valley. Over the previous two hours or so the going had changed from being reasonably flat into rising steeply into the mountains. The river had also narrowed and was now flowing much faster. In several places he encountered rapids, deep gullies and one or two waterfalls. However, all these obstacles were negotiated without too much difficulty.

About half an hour before nightfall he found a convenient place to rest up for the night which gave him a good view back the way he had come. He decided that it was safe enough to light a fire and cook himself something to eat. It was as he was collecting wood for his fire that he found signs of horses having passed that way in the not too distant past. He calculated that the tracks were made by four horses. At least he now knew that the Indian policemen were ahead of him.

Not knowing exactly how far ahead the Indian policemen were bothered him slightly. Wherever possible he liked to know the location of any potential adversary and he considered these Indians as such.

It seemed to him that the summit of the hill he was climbing was no more than about 200 feet above him, although he realized that probably meant a journey of about a mile. Having weighed up the difficulties, he decided to forget about his fire for the moment and climb to the top in the hope of being able to see exactly where and how far ahead the Indians were. Having already unsaddled his horse he decided to leave her and make the journey on foot. He took his rifle just in case he should need it, which he doubted but he was, as ever, very cautious.

It proved to be a little further than he had expected but eventually he found himself at what he believed to be the highest point. By that time it was completely dark but his years of experience in similar conditions had sharpened many of his natural senses, including his eyesight, which now made it possible for him to make out most of his surroundings and even the vaguest outline of distant hills.

His journey did not turn out to be a waste of time. From what he could see he sensed that he had reached the Yellow River Valley. From that point onwards it seemed that the land widened out into a wide, fairly flat valley and he was even able to see the merest hint of starlight reflecting in the river. More importantly, as far as he was concerned, he was able to see the flames of a fire. He guessed that the fire was about two miles away, three at the most.

Now he was satisfied and was able to plan his strategy for the next day accordingly. As he turned to make his way back to his horse, he stopped and stared back down the valley he had just negotiated. There was no doubt about it, another fire had been lit, this time possibly four miles away. Four miles was a long way for any man to see but in the almost total darkness his keen eyes were able to pick out even the faintest glimmer of light. He now knew where both his adversaries were. Four white men to the south and four Indian policemen to the north. The danger the white men presented was something he knew about but the danger presented by the Indian policemen was an entirely unknown quantity.

He did have second thoughts about lighting his own fire but he was reasonably convinced that Carl Edwards and his men would not be able to see it and he knew it to be out of sight to the Indian policemen. Apart from the need to cook his food, the temperature was beginning to drop quite rapidly and warmth was going to be vital. Men had been known to freeze to death even in the heat of summer in both the high mountains and, strangely enough, out in the desert.

He was on his way the following morning as soon as dawn broke and he felt that Edwards and his men had probably done the same. He made no attempt to hide the fact that he had been there, leaving the still-warm embers of his fire. There did not seem much point in even trying to cover his tracks, Edwards would be well aware that he was not too far in front. However, the Indian policemen would not be aware that he was behind them and he was not too anxious to make his presence known. He proceeded with great caution.

As expected, once he had reached the summit of the hill, he found himself looking along a wide valley. The river had now widened again and meandered along the floor of the valley. Although the valley was relatively free of trees at that point, it became more thickly wooded further up and from then on was thick woodland as far as the eye could see. His progress now became much slower and more cautious. He had no idea exactly where the Indian policemen would be and he did not want to chance upon them by accident.

Half an hour later he came across the remains of their camp and it seemed that they had left not more than half an hour earlier. He gathered this much from the fact that the fire was still hot and the still-warm relics of their breakfast – a small deer carcass – was still on a spit over the fire. In fact there was enough left of the deer for him to have a sizeable meal, which he did.

In reality he was wasting time, he wanted to give the Indians time to get further in front. He did not really want to encounter them at all at this point, his goal now was to locate the so-called renegade Indian village before they did and warn Jimmy Two Rivers.

However, his now much slower rate of progress meant that Carl Edwards and his men were almost certainly closing the gap on him and he did not take too kindly to the idea of being trapped between the Indian policemen and Edwards.

The signs left by the Indian policemen were plain to see. They were obviously not expecting anyone to be following them and had made no attempt to hide their tracks. Brogan followed these tracks for about two miles before deciding that they were becoming a little too fresh for his comfort.

He had also been thinking of ways to locate the Indian village and had reached the conclusion that he might stand a better chance of seeing signs from higher up the side of the valley. He found a place which appeared to offer the best chance of climbing higher. Bearing in mind the men following him, Brogan took care to hide signs of his departure from the main trail. He had no idea just how good Edwards and his men were at tracking and was not prepared to risk them being unable to read the signs. He had made that mistake several times early on in his career as a saddletramp and those mistakes had nearly cost him his life on several occasions.

An hour later Brogan was almost at the top of the

valley side and gazing down on the now thick woodland, looking for any indication of a village and also for signs of the Indian policemen and Carl Edwards. There were no signs of anything or anyone. He slowly continued his ride along what was fairly open ground just above the main treeline.

Half an hour later, still having seen nothing, he suddenly stopped and listened intently. He was quite certain that there was someone not far ahead. He dismounted and placed his finger against his lip in an effort to tell his horse that she must remain perfectly quiet. The horse gave him a baleful, pitying look and almost contemptuously lowered her head and started to eat some grass. Brogan took his rifle and continued forward on foot.

About fifty yards further on he came across a large outcrop of rock below which, if his senses proved accurate – which they usually did – he knew he would find whoever had alerted him. He crept slowly to the end of the outcrop and looked down, taking care that he could not be seen.

A feeling of dismay overcame him as he looked down. Fifty or so feet below him the four Indian policemen were sat on the end of another outcrop overlooking the valley floor. They had obviously arrived at the same idea as himself and had taken to higher ground in an attempt to locate the village.

They did not seem to be in any particular hurry and were plainly not afraid of being overheard. They chatted and laughed among themselves for some considerable time. Eventually it appeared that they were about to move on. Unfortunately the direction they seemed to favour was also the direction which Brogan would have to follow. Suddenly one of them called to the others and pointed downwards. All four grabbed their rifles and waited.

It seemed to be a long time before anyone appeared and when they did, Brogan was not at all surprised to see Carl Edwards and his men. He was now thankful that he had taken the precaution of covering his tracks since it was obvious that Edwards had followed those made by the Indians.

For their part, the Indian policemen did not seem too pleased to see their visitors and at first an angry exchange of words passed between them. Brogan could make out odd words but was unable to make much sense of the conversation. However, he did hear his name mentioned together with something about a $1,000 reward. It was not much but it served to tell Brogan exactly what was happening.

Very clever, Mr Edwards, Brogan said to himself. You spin some yarn about me bein' worth a thousand dollars an' that way you get them to do all the work of lookin' for me. My bet is that if they do find me an' manage to take me alive, you'll move in, kill them an' kill me too – if you can. Well, gentlemen, as they say, forewarned is forearmed.

For a few moments, Brogan even considered the possibility of shooting all or some of them. There was no doubt about it, he could certainly remove at least two of them before they had a chance to find cover. The problem was which two? He somewhat reluctantly abandoned the idea. Not because he had any qualms about killing any of them – he could easily justify his own conscience on that matter – but the survivors would almost certainly join forces and track him down. Again, it was not the thought of at least six men trailing him but more the realization that in killing them now he was simply going to make life even more difficult for himself. Life was difficult enough without adding to his problems when there was no need.

He remained where he was and eventually the four Indians continued on their way. When they were out of sight the four white men laughed and congratulated each other. For a few seconds Brogan toyed with the butt of his rifle but shook his head and abandoned the idea.

It appeared that Edwards and his men were prepared to remain where they were for the moment and there was little Brogan could do other than wait. About half an hour after the Indian policemen had departed, Carl Edwards ordered his men to mount up and they followed. Brogan waited until they were well clear before returning to his horse.

'It's gettin' kinda crowded up here,' he said to his horse. 'If I had any sense I'd get the hell out of it an' forget all about Two Rivers.' His horse nodded. 'My trouble is I ain't got no sense.' Again his horse nodded. 'I might've guessed you'd agree. OK, so what do we do now, follow 'em?' This time she shook her head. 'They won't be expectin' me to be followin', they must think I'm up ahead somewhere. We follow.'

Brogan quickly discovered that he did not need to look for tracks, he could hear Edwards and his men talking from some considerable distance and he continued to follow them for about another hour at least. Suddenly he realized that they had stopped talking amongst themselves and were apparently talking to someone else. That someone else could only be the Indian policemen. Once again he left his horse after instructing her to remain quiet and went forward on foot.

He found a thick clump of trees from where he looked along a small ridge and saw, as he had expected, the four white men and the four Indian policemen. It was obvious that they were discussing something in the distance which Brogan could not see but which he assumed to be signs of the Indian village. He had little alternative but to wait, watch and listen. Eventually all eight men mounted their horses and disappeared down the ridge. Brogan gave them a few minutes to get well clear before going to the ridge to see what they had been discussing.

What he did see were several thin plumes of smoke rising almost vertically in the still air about two miles away down in the valley floor amongst the trees. He had no doubt that he had discovered the Indian village. His problem now was how to get to the village and warn them of what was about to happen. He did not know what plans had been made to attack the village, which made it all the more important that he should get there first. He calculated that there were about another two hours until sunset.

Since Edwards and the Indian policemen had apparently descended on to the valley floor south of the village, he decided that the only way he could reach the village without the risk of being seen was to carry on along the side of the valley and go into the village from the north. He simply had to hope that the attack would not take place before he could reach them.

Squaw Hunters

After retrieving his horse, Brogan made his way along the side of the valley as quickly as he could, stopping a couple of times to check the location of the village. However, when he decided to move down the valley side, he discovered that it was not so easy.

He encountered a series of cliffs, not particularly high, but high enough to force him into quite a lengthy detour on each occasion. The first three cliffs were negotiated, if slowly, with relative ease but the final cliff with a drop of about 100 feet proved to be a different matter and there was no obvious detour or way down. He was forced along a tortuous route further north than he would have liked. Eventually he found himself at the top of a large, fairly steep scree of loose rock which seemed to offer the only chance of descent.

He dismounted and coaxed his horse to the edge of the scree, telling her that all she had to do was concentrate on staying upright. The horse was obviously not very happy with the idea and at first resisted strongly. Eventually however, after a lot of coaxing and pulling, both of them were sliding steadily down the scree.

The horse apparently managed to remain upright but Brogan suddenly found himself releasing the reins and losing his balance and sliding with ever-increasing speed and pain downwards. He did not really remember reaching the bottom but realized that he had when loose rock started to pile up both on and around him. After something of a struggle he managed to pull himself clear.

His whole body ached and was apparently covered in blood from numerous grazes and scratches, but he was otherwise unhurt. He did not appear to have suffered any broken bones. His horse too had several grazes and scratches to her legs, but she too seemed otherwise uninjured.

'Sorry about that, old girl,' he apologized. His horse simply snorted and tossed her head. 'Still, we're down now. Do you feel like carryin' on?' She shook her head violently. 'Well we have to,' he grunted as he mounted up. 'That village shouldn't be too far away.'

Much as Brogan would have liked to force his horse into an unaccustomed gallop, he did not. This was partly because he did not want to aggravate any injuries she might have and partly because the forest floor was littered with fallen trees and branches, most of which were covered in slippery moss and could have resulted in far more serious injury both to himself and his horse had she slipped. As it was he was forced to dismount and lead her round obtacles several times.

Reaching the village took far longer than he had expected but eventually he found himself looking at several rough huts made from branches, set on a small hillock in one of the few clearings. Activity in the village appeared perfectly normal, which obviously meant that he had reached them before Edwards and the Indian policemen.

At first he hesitated, uncertain what kind of reception he would receive and he spent some time looking for Jimmy Two Rivers. There was no guarantee that Two Rivers would be in the village and the probability was that he would receive anything but a friendly greeting if Two Rivers was not there to vouch for him. There was not even any guarantee that Two Rivers would vouch for him. Eventually he decided that the only way to find out was to go into the village.

Brogan's arrival caused near panic, particularly amongst the women and children. Mothers hastily gathered their offspring and ran into the woods and most of the men ran to their huts and returned with various ancient weapons, even spears and bows and arrows. An arrow thudded into a tree close to Brogan's head but he resisted the temptation to go for his guns. Such an action would, he knew, certainly result in his death. He raised his hands and, using his knees, urged his horse forward.

Very quickly he was completely surrounded and herded to the centre of the village. The mood of the men was such that he knew it would take only the slightest movement which could be interpreted as hostile for them to kill him. He raised his hands a little higher.

'Anyone speak English?' he asked. Most of them said nothing, simply staring threateningly at him. Eventually one old man came forward.

'I speak English,' said the man. 'What are you doing here?'

'I come to find one called Jimmy Two Rivers,' replied Brogan, keeping his hands well above his head. 'You are in great danger.'

'We know of nobody called Jimmy Two Rivers,' said the man.

'You must,' said Brogan. 'He told me himself this was where he was heading.'

'Why should he tell you this?' demanded the old man.

'I found him and some of your people at a farm,'

said Brogan. 'The men from Cottonwood they call squaw hunters had killed ten of your men. They had removed their heads. I found them not long after it had happened.'

'And why should you care?' demanded the old man again. 'The white man does not care what happens to Indians.'

'It's a long story,' said Brogan. 'Do you mind if I lower my hands?' The old man nodded but raised the spear he was carrying. 'Two Rivers can vouch for what I say. Is he here?'

'He is not here,' said another, younger man stepping forward. 'He has taken some men hunting. He will return soon. He told me of a white man who found the farm who did not seem to hate us. You are that man?'

'I am that man,' confirmed Brogan.

At that moment several women came out of the forest where they had taken refuge and one of them spoke to both men. The old man nodded and shouted an order to the others and immediately all weapons were lowered.

'She was in the barn when you arrived,' said the old man. 'She confirms that you are the man. What is this danger of which you speak?'

At that moment a group of young men arrived, carrying two large deer between them. Their initial instinct was to drop the carcasses and take up their weapons but the old man spoke to them; they lowered the weapons but they remained suspicious. Two more young men came out of the forest, both carrying several large birds. One of these Brogan recognized as Jimmy Two Rivers.

Words were exchanged between the old man and

Two Rivers, who came forward and nodded at Brogan.

'I had not thought to see you again,' said Two Rivers. 'Why do you come here? You are not welcome, no white man is welcome.'

'That's what I like,' said Brogan. 'A nice, friendly greetin'. I've been tryin' to tell your people here that you are in great danger. There are four men from the Indian police who have been sent to kill you in particular. They are now with four white men from Cottonwood. I wouldn't be surprised if you know the white men. I think they are the men who attacked your farm.'

'Why are the white men here?' asked Two Rivers.

'They are lookin' for me,' said Brogan. 'They want to kill me.'

'And the Indian policemen, do they want to kill you?'

'They probably do now,' said Brogan. 'That's not why they came up here though. I don't know if you know it or not, but there's a reward out on you. I think it's five hundred dollars. They came after you and the reward. I overheard the sheriff at Cottonwood tellin' them to come here. I thought I'd better warn you.'

'Why should you bother?' asked Two Rivers. 'You are different from most white men, this I know, but why should you risk your life for me?'

'Let's just say I didn't like what I saw back in Cottonwood,' said Brogan. 'I saw children an' some grown men bein' sold. The children were sold into what they call apprenticeships and the men were sold simply because they had no jobs. I gather they have to serve four months as labourers. You said that

I would learn the truth and then forget you. Well, I learned the truth but I didn't forget you.'

Two Rivers laughed. 'This is true, that is what I said. Those men, they serve four months and as soon as they are released they are arrested again because they have no work and are sold again. Some have lived this way for many years. They are never free.' He looked up at the sky and nodded. 'I will send men into the forest to watch for these men. I do not believe they will attack tonight, but we will be ready for them in the morning. Unfortunately we do not have modern weapons, but there are over twenty men and youths who can fight.'

'You've got two modern guns if you want 'em,' said Brogan. 'The one condition is that I use 'em.'

'You are truly not as other white men,' said Two Rivers, smiling. 'Very well, my friend, we either live or die together.'

SEVEN

There was not much sleep in the Indian village that night but as the night wore on it became increasingly obvious to Brogan that there would be no attack using darkness as cover. At least this lack of action gave him time to think and to organize the Indians as best he could.

Under Brogan's guidance, the few firearms the Indians possessed and the men to use them were placed at strategic points on the approaches to the village. They were reinforced by men armed with spears and bows and arrows although Brogan had little faith in their effectiveness.

Most of the women and a few of the older children were drafted in and assigned the task of ensuring that what were mainly muzzle-loading rifles were kept loaded. The Indians might have had enough guns to deal with eight men, who were each armed with modern repeater rifles and handguns, by sheer weight of numbers but, like the spears and bows and arrows, he had serious reservations as to the effectiveness of the ancient weapons owned by the Indians or their ability to use them effectively.

He also very quickly discovered that there was a

chronic shortage of ball-shot and powder. Powder in particular was in very short supply and the varying bore of the rifles the Indians possessed meant that some sizes of shot were also in short supply. However, much as he would have wished it otherwise, Brogan simply had to make best use of what he had. He had been in similar positions before and had somehow managed to come through. He only hoped that he could pull off what appeared to be a miracle on this occasion.

Bearing in mind the shortage of powder and shot, Brogan, with the aid of Jimmy Two Rivers as interpreter, did his best to impress upon everyone that every shot was vital and that no bullets or shot were to be wasted shooting at anything other than a clear target. Although all seemed to appreciate this need, he had doubts as to the ability of most of the men to remain calm under attack. Already some of them were showing signs of panic.

He expressed these fears to Jimmy Two Rivers who simply shrugged and said that everyone was prepared to die rather than submit. Submission was not something Brogan was prepared to consider. He knew that there would be very little mercy shown by their attackers.

Shortly after midnight one of the men sent out to locate the Indian policemen and Carl Edwards returned with the news that they were camped about half a mile away but that they appeared to have settled down for the night, although one of them had been posted as look-out.

Jimmy Two Rivers was all for striking first there and then and whilst this probably would have taken them by surprise, Brogan managed to convince Two

Rivers that in the dark they could not be certain of killing everyone. He pointed out that it would need only one survivor to get back to Cottonwood to have the army brought in. If that happened he knew that the Indians and their village would be totally wiped out. So, Brogan gave instructions that all the men now under his command should remain where they were, although he did agree for them to get what sleep they could provided they posted at least one look-out. For his part, Brogan was past sleep and constantly toured the area checking and double checking.

At certain points he arranged for sharp stakes to be placed in the ground but, as with their other weapons, he did not really have much faith in this as a means of protecting the village since he thought it most unlikely that they would attack on horseback. Having their horses brought down would place them at a distinct disadvantage and he had no doubt that they knew this as well as he did.

Having established exactly where their likely assailants were, he also ordered that two men should keep a constant watch on them and report any movement. As the first rays of dawn filtered through the forest, one of the look-outs returned to report that they were awake and apparently making preparation to attack.

The one thing that Brogan had established in his own mind, was that there were only two probable avenues of attack. The obvious route was directly along a fairly narrow track and Brogan doubted if they would use it. The second and more likely was through a thickly wooded area just to the right of the trail. This would provide the attackers with plenty of cover whilst at the same time giving them a clear view of the village.

He had no doubt that at least one of the Indian policemen had also checked on the village and the approaches to it. What he did not know was whether they knew he was there. Not that it mattered that much. If they did know they probably thought it a good thing in that they could take both him and Two Rivers at the same time.

A short time after the first look-out had returned, the second appeared and informed them that all eight men had left their camp and were heading their way. The word spread very quickly and Brogan made one last tour of the defences. He sighed heavily and knew that luck rather than skill was going to play a large part in any possible success.

Having done his best with what men and arms they had, Brogan placed himself behind a fallen tree and waited. He knew that his guns were going to play a very important part in the impending fight and he had made certain that he at least had plenty of ammunition. Half an hour later, somewhat to his surprise, there was still no sign of any attack.

Had it been only Carl Edwards and his men, Brogan was quite certain that the attack would have taken place by then, the men simply riding in with guns blazing. However, the presence of the Indian policemen put a very different light on things. They would be much more wary and he sensed that even at that moment several pairs of eyes were looking at them from the forest, weighing up all the options.

The initial attack, when it did happen, took even Brogan by surprise, which was something that happened very rarely. He cursed himself for not having considered it. The morning sun had still not penetrated the forest floor to any great extent and it was still very dark.

Quite suddenly and from a direction that Brogan had not anticipated – behind the village – a ball of fire, probably a flaming arrow, flew through the air and landed on the roof of one of the huts. The flames spread rapidly. This was followed by several more flying balls of flame, each one accurately finding a target on one of the many huts. The immediate effect was probably exactly what had been intended. Panic, particularly amongst the women and children.

In the space of no more than two minutes people were screaming and running about in all directions, desperately looking for places of safety. The few ponies the Indians owned also broke out of a small paddock and disappeared into the forest. With a certain amount of smug satisfaction Brogan noticed that his own horse, although tossing her head and fretting a little, remained where she was.

Brogan did his best to calm everyone down but his words fell upon deaf ears and he was finally forced to stand aside and watch helplessly. He was eventually joined by Jimmy Two Rivers and several other young men who had deserted the positions to which they had been assigned.

'Just what they wanted,' he shouted at the men. 'Cause panic an' then all they have to do is clear up. That was just a diversion, get back, they'll be comin' in any moment now.'

Jimmy Two Rivers looked at the few remaining men and shrugged. 'We cannot hold out against them,' he said. 'We must retreat and hide in the forest. There at least we have some chance. See, the women and children and some of the men are already running into the forest. We must join them.'

'Where you'll be picked off one by one,' grated Brogan. 'Your best bet is to stand an' fight right here.'

In answer to his observation about being picked off one by one, there was a sudden burst of gunfire, this time from the direction he had expected the attack to take place. He saw at least three men and one woman fall to the ground, where they remained ominously still.

There were a few shots from the direction the flaming arrows had come from, followed by several cries of pain which indicated that that direction had also been cut off. However, this did not stop even more women and children running for the imagined safety of the trees. There were several loud screams as some of those fleeing were plainly being dealt with, probably being stabbed or even having their throats cut.

'Your only chance now is to stand an' fight,' shouted Brogan. 'Find some cover an' wait for 'em. Remember, only shoot when you have a clear target and make sure you shoot to kill.'

Reluctantly, it seemed, the men agreed and dispersed behind what cover they could find. Brogan joined Jimmy Two Rivers behind the fallen tree. An ominous silence descended on the forest.

'You don't stand a chance, McNally!' Carl Edwards suddenly called out. 'You an' Two Rivers give yourselves up an' the others can go free.'

'I think we'd both rather die fightin',' called Brogan. 'You don't intend to take us alive.'

'Maybe not,' called Edwards, 'but at least the others will live. If you don't, I can guarantee that every man, woman an' child will be killed. Do you want their deaths on your conscience?'

'If I'm dead too, I won't have no conscience to bother me, will I?' said Brogan. 'No deal, Edwards. If you want me an' Two Rivers so bad you'll just have to come an' get us.'

'I'd say time was on our side,' replied Edwards, laughing. 'OK, we ain't stupid enough to think we can take you without some of us bein' killed so we ain't even goin' to try. I've seen you in action so I know you can shoot. We got us some mighty fine-lookin' women an' girls now. You can listen to us havin' a good time with 'em. You can sit there an' rot for a while. We've got you surrounded an' we can pick you off one at a time.' His comment was reinforced as a single shot slammed into the shoulder of one of the Indians who had foolishly exposed himself too much. 'That's one more out of action,' gloated Edwards. 'One down an' I reckon only twelve more, maybe thirteen, to go. I hope you are the last one, McNally, I want to see you die real slow an' real painful. Oh, an' just in case you're thinkin' of makin' a run for it, just remember you're surrounded.'

There followed a lewd laugh from Edwards and once again silence descended but was suddenly broken as a woman screamed. Neither Brogan nor Jimmy Two Rivers needed anyone to tell them what was happening.

'We must do something!' hissed Two Rivers. 'I can't just stay here and listen to our women being abused.'

'I'm thinkin'!' grated Brogan. 'Right now though, I don't think there's much we can do. Have you got any bright ideas?'

'Perhaps if I give myself up they will be satisfied,' said Two Rivers. 'It is me they want. I could agree with them that I will give myself up in return for the safety of the others.'

'Oh, sure,' said Brogan, sarcastically. 'I can guarantee they'll agree to that but as soon as they have you they'll just slaughter everyone else. They want me too, remember, an' I ain't about to simply walk out with my hands up. As long as you an' me are alive I reckon the women an' children will be safe enough. They'll keep 'em alive because they think they need somethin' to bargain with.' There was another scream from the forest.

'Perhaps they will keep them alive,' said Two Rivers, 'but that will not stop them using the women.'

'Maybe not,' agreed Brogan. 'But at least they'll still be alive. Now shut up an' let me think. It ain't just your hide I'm thinkin' about, I ain't ready to die just yet.'

'Then perhaps you made a mistake in helping us,' said Two Rivers. Brogan grunted something about agreeing with him.

Brogan did not think for one moment that all their assailants were now involved in the abuse of the women and to test this he slowly raised his hat on the end of a stick. He was right; an accurate shot sent the hat spinning from the stick. He managed to recover the hat and ruefully poked his finger through the hole.

'Good job my head wasn't in it,' he said. 'Still, it

tells me one thing for sure, he's over there behind that big oak. I'd say he was the only one on this side though. I need to know how many there are behind us.'

'Then I will find out, my friend,' said Two Rivers. 'I will run across to that large tree . . .' He pointed to a large oak tree about fifty yards away at the far side of the clearing. 'I will draw their fire and you will be able to see where they are and how many there are.'

'Don't be a bloody fool!' said Brogan. 'You'll never make it.'

'At least I will have died trying,' said Two Rivers with a broad smile. 'I cannot just wait here to be killed.' He did not give Brogan time to either talk him out of it or stop him. He was suddenly running across the clearing.

Brogan counted four shots, two of which were from the man hidden by the oak tree in front of them. He was also quite certain that the other two shots were fired by only one man from the forest behind the village.

Jimmy Two Rivers was extremely swift on his feet and this combined with his zigzagging across the open space obviously prevented either man getting a clear shot and it appeared that he reached the tree without obvious injury.

The sudden departure of Two Rivers, their leader, plainly unnerved the remaining men and quite suddenly they too were racing across the open space. There were shots from both the man in front and the man behind and four of the Indians crashed to the ground. One of them was plainly not killed and screamed out in agony as he writhed about. Brogan had no choice but to leave him where he was.

'Bloody fools!' he muttered as the remaining men sought cover behind the oak tree with Jimmy Two Rivers. 'What the hell am I supposed to do now?'

The sudden activity had also brought Carl Edwards back. 'Looks like you're on your own now, McNally,' he gloated. 'Your friends have deserted you. I could've told you that'd happen. They're all cowards. Gettin' our hands on Two Rivers shouldn't be no problem now an' you can stay where you are for all I care. You'll have a good view of what happens to renegade Indians in these parts.'

'You want me too, remember,' said Brogan.

'You can wait,' replied Edwards. 'First we eliminate everybody else an' then we deal with you.'

The movement of some bushes opposite Brogan told him that even then men were moving round the village. Their objective was quite obvious. The few remaining Indians capable of putting up any resistance were now all crowded around a solitary large oak tree on the far side of the clearing and he was quite certain that it would be little more than a matter of time before they were all eliminated,, His mind worked quickly.

With attention now focused on the Indians under the oak tree, Brogan pulled himself along the ground flat on his stomach, half expecting to feel a bullet thudding into his back at any moment.

From where he was, it was about twenty yards to the forest. In that short distance there were three bodies and his hope was that anyone watching might not notice an extra body. Very slowly he inched his way forward, still expecting that fatal shot. He had covered about ten yards when there was a sudden burst of gunfire from the far side of the clearing.

The attack on Jimmy Two Rivers and his men had started. Brogan weighed up the chances of his reaching the forest and decided that that moment was as good a time as any to make a dash for it.

A shot thudded into a tree close by his head as Brogan reached the forest where he crouched, looked and listened. He could hear someone shouting but not what was being said, the sound of shooting drowning everything out. Suddenly the shooting stopped and a voice called out to tell Edwards that Brogan had managed to escape to the forest. Carl Edwards' choice of words to describe the incompetence of his companion left little room for doubt as to his feelings on the matter.

There was another shout followed by two shots, the shout informing Edwards that the Indians who had been captured were making a break for it. Edwards' response was to order the man to forget about the Indians and concentrate on finding Brogan.

With the apparent escape of the Indian women and children Brogan breathed a sigh of relief. It meant that there was one less problem for him to worry about. However, Brogan's normally highly attuned senses were not much use to him. There was so much noise from almost every direction that it was impossible for him to pin-point any of the attackers.

For some minutes he remained where he was looking and listening. The sudden crashing of a body through the undergrowth almost had him shooting one of the escaping women. He realized who it was just in time and gave the woman a piece of his mind and a few of his more choice words.

Very slowly the sounds of fleeing Indians subsided and he moved a little closer to the clearing in the hope of establishing what had happened to Jimmy Two Rivers and the remaining Indian men.

It was plain that the attack on Two Rivers had, for the moment, been abandoned although when one of the Indians temporarily broke his cover a shot was fired, telling both the Indians and Brogan that at least one man had been left to make sure that they did not escape. Satisfied, Brogan moved a little deeper into the forest.

He slowly made his way towards where Edwards had been reported as having made camp for the night. His aim was quite simple; he intended, if possible, to scatter their horses. About fifteen minutes later he was looking down on a small hollow containing the eight horses. There did not appear to be anyone guarding them.

Slowly and very cautiously he made his way amongst the horses and unhitched them. There was still no immediate sign of anyone and he slowly led all eight horses away, ensuring that at least two animals were always between him and any possible gun. He was very surprised when, after about another ten minutes, he had not been challenged.

His plan to scatter the horses changed when he found himself at the entrance to a deep gully thickly lined with trees and scrub. He led the animals well into the gully and hitched them to various trees. As he left the gully he did his best to hide the tracks the horses had made and was eventually satisfied that all but the best of trackers would not be able to follow the signs. He then made his way back towards the village.

Squaw Hunters

Apart from the occasional shot which he assumed was aimed at Jimmy Two Rivers and the remaining Indian men, there was almost complete silence. This silence suited Brogan very well. It meant that his ears in particular would be able to pick up even the slightest movement.

He did hear the sounds of someone making their way through the bushes but they were too far away for him to do anything at that moment. Slowly he made his way towards the sound. Quite suddenly the abilities of the Indian policemen as masters of the forest hit him hard.

He had not heard the man until he looked up to see a blue-uniformed body hurtling towards him. There was not enough time to shoot and the Indian policeman thudded into him, sending him crashing to the ground. He caught the flash of steel as a knife swung at him.

The knife missed as Brogan rolled under the man and he was very quickly on his feet. His immediate problem was that in the onslaught he had lost both his Colt and his Winchester and he found himself facing the grinning face of his attacker, who was about to raise his rifle.

Brogan acted very swiftly and the knife he always carried in his belt flashed towards the Indian and thudded into his chest. The policeman looked more startled than hurt but very slowly his sneering grin changed to disbelief The gun in his hand slowly dropped to the ground to be followed by the Indian. Brogan wiped his brow and bent down to remove the knife from the man's chest. There was a brief attempt by the Indian to grab Brogan but this ended when the knife slid across the man's throat.

'As the man said,' Brogan said to himself. 'One down, seven to go.' He picked up his guns and those of the Indian policeman and continued towards the village. Once again silence descended.

A few minutes later there was a shout. Somebody had discovered that the horses were missing. Brogan could not resist answering.

'No horses an' now there's only seven of you, Edwards,' he called. 'I just took out one of your Indian friends. The odds are gettin' better all the time.'

'It's still seven against one, McNally,' called Edwards from some distance away but at least it told Brogan roughly where Edwards was. 'You can't've taken the horses very far, we'll soon find 'em.'

'They could be anywhere now,' said Brogan. 'I scattered 'em in the forest. It could take you days to find 'em.'

'Damn you, McNally!' shouted Edwards. 'The horses can wait. From now on you're goin' to find out just how a deer feels like when it's bein' hunted.'

'I ain't no deer,' reminded Brogan. 'I'd say the odds were less than seven to one. There's at least one of you keepin' Two Rivers an' his men pinned down.'

'Don't rely on it,' shouted Edwards.

Brogan decided that it was time to shut up and move away. He had no doubt that his location had been worked out by one of the remaining Indian policemen if by nobody else. He climbed a small bank just in time.

Below him, where he had just been, a figure appeared. His only surprise was that it was not that of an Indian policeman but one of Edwards' men.

Afterwards he realized that he should not have been surprised. An Indian would not have exposed himself so readily. Brogan did not hesitate; his rifle spat its message of death and the man fell to the ground, blood oozing from his temple.

'One more out of action,' called Brogan. 'One of yours this time, Edwards. That leaves just six of you. Like I say, the odds are gettin' better all the time.' He moved on again.

Brogan was brought up short by a sudden burst of gunfire and a cry for help from one of Edwards' men. He managed to hear that Jimmy Two Rivers and the remaining Indians had made a break for it. He did hear something about three of them being killed but he had no idea if Two Rivers was one of these or not.

'I guess that leaves just you an' us, McNally,' called Edwards. 'We can clear up the others later.'

This time, Brogan decided to remain silent. In his experience, not knowing where someone was very often unnerved men like Edwards. He was not too sure if it would have the same effect upon the Indian policemen.

EIGHT

For some considerable time, silence descended on the forest and Brogan elected to remain where he was. He took the opportunity to consider his position and still eventually came to the conclusion that the Indians needed his help. It would have been a relatively easy matter for him to have simply ridden out and saved his own skin. However, if somewhat against his better judgement, he decided that if he were to desert them now they would certainly be wiped out.

All the time he listened for the slightest of sounds which might indicate where any of the remaining six men were but it appeared that they too were playing the waiting game. There was not even the sound or sight of birds; apparently they had all been frightened away by the noise.

After what seemed a very long time, Brogan suddenly became aware of someone moving slowly in his direction. The direction from which the sounds came rather surprised him, they came from a location opposite to what he had expected. He eased himself round, his back against a tree, his rifle at the ready, and waited.

The sounds, slight as they were, were plainly made by more than one man and Brogan estimated that there were at least three of them. He waited until he saw several bushes move just below him. He was about to shoot when he realized just in time that they were not any of the men with Carl Edwards, they were Indians from the village.

'You almost got yourselves killed,' hissed Brogan.

'Do not shoot, my friend,' the unmistakable voice of Jimmy Two Rivers whispered in reply. 'As you have probably heard, we managed to escape and have come to help you. We knew you were somewhere nearby. We could not leave you to fight alone.'

'Over here,' whispered Brogan. 'I thought you'd high-tailed it.'

'Three of us agreed that we had to come back and help you,' said Two Rivers. 'The others have fled into the forest but they will not be too far away. I think they will come if we need them.'

'Then you have a darned sight more faith in them than I have,' muttered Brogan as the three Indians appeared. Of the three, only one possessed a decent repeater rifle, Two Rivers and the other one carried ancient muzzle loaders. Brogan tossed the rifle he had taken from the Indian policeman to Two Rivers and the pistol to the other man.

'We do not have much ammunition,' said Two Rivers. 'Only what is in these guns. Perhaps it will be enough.'

'And I don't have the right bullets for them guns I just gave you,' said Brogan. 'There's two bodies back there, it's a wonder you didn't see 'em. One is one of the policemen and the other one of Edwards' men. Those guns belonged to the policeman. One of you ought to go and find the bodies an' get the other guns and as many bullets as you can. Just head straight back, you can't miss 'em.'

Two Rivers spoke to his men and one of them nodded and disappeared. He returned a few minutes later carrying another rifle, a hand gun, two belts of bullets and a big smile.

'Now we are ready for anything,' said Two Rivers. 'We have good weapons and plenty of bullets. I heard that you have sent their horses into the forest, so they cannot escape.'

'Somethin' like that,' admitted Brogan, not prepared to tell Two Rivers where the horses were. 'Don't underestimate them though, I reckon them policemen know a thing or two.'

Two Rivers spat on the ground. 'Shoshone!' he hissed. 'Sworn enemies of the Lakota. They are plainsmen, we are used to this kind of country, they are not.'

'I don't care who they are or what they are,' said Brogan. 'I still say they know a thing or two about fightin' in this kind of country. Still, I'm glad to have you along, I need all the help I can get. What about your women an' children?'

'They will be safe,' assured Two Rivers. 'Already they are scattered throughout the forest, they will never be found.'

'I wouldn't be too sure about that,' said Brogan. 'All it needs is somebody to get back to Cottonwood and tell 'em what's happened an' I'll guarantee the army will soon be out here in force. If the army do come I wouldn't give anythin' for your chances. From what I can gather there's nobody who'd give a damn what happened to you but they sure as hell would want to do somethin' if word gets out that you've killed any white man or Indian policeman.'

'Then we have to be sure that nobody returns to Cottonwood,' said Two Rivers. 'We will hunt them down and kill them all. That way nobody will ever know what happened to them.'

'I guess that's exactly what they're thinkin',' said Brogan. 'Huntin' you all down. Right now though I reckon I'm top of the wanted list. This could be interestin' although I can think of plenty other things I'd rather be doin' at this moment. I can't help wonderin' if you came lookin' for me to help me or 'cos you still need me to help you.'

'At this moment, my friend,' Two Rivers grinned, 'I think it is that we are in need of each other.'

'I reckon I can manage on my own,' grunted Brogan. 'In fact I might be better off on my own. Still, I guess in a way you're right. Welcome aboard.'

'I do not understand,' said Two Rivers. 'What is this welcome aboard?'

Brogan smiled and nodded. 'Yeh, I guess it don't mean much to you stuck out here in the middle of the country, you don't get many ships out here. It's an old naval expression I heard when I was a kid back in Seattle. Seattle's on the coast, it's a big port where lots of boats from all over the world go to.'

'That must be what they call the sea,' said Two Rivers. 'I have heard there is such a thing. Water for as far as a man can see and could never reach the end of and yet cannot be drunk. I have never understood why that is. Surely water is water.'

'It's got too much salt in it,' said Brogan.

'I still do not understand,' said Two Rivers. 'However, that is unimportant for the moment. We are here to help you, my friend. Thanks to you we now have good guns. What would you have us do now?'

'You do exactly what I tell you to do,' said Brogan. 'You only shoot when I tell you. I don't care what happens, you do exactly what I tell you to do unless somebody is tryin' to kill you. Do you understand?'

Two Rivers spoke to his companions who nodded. 'We understand,' he said.

'I hope you do,' said Brogan. 'Right now we have to find out exactly where they are. Just remember, if we do see anybody, no shootin' unless I say so.'

'I don't like it,' Carl Edwards said to his companions. 'I don't like it at all. McNally ain't like any other man I ever met. For a start he's the fastest an' most accurate I've ever seen an' I have this feelin' that he's probably more at home in this kind of country than a grizzly bear. We could look for him for the rest of our lives an' never find him an' he could be no more'n a few yards away.'

'So what do we do?' asked one of the Indian policemen. 'Already he has killed two of us and he could kill the rest of us at any time. It is a pity he was ever allowed to reach the forest.'

'That was Frank's fault,' muttered Edwards. 'His fault an' now he's paid for it. McNally says he's killed him an' I for one believe him.'

'He has also killed my brother,' said the Indian policeman. 'I must avenge his death.'

'Brother!' queried Edwards. 'You mean he really was your actual brother?'

'Since we both had the same mother, he was my brother,' said the Indian.

'OK, I know how you must feel,' said Edwards. 'The thing is I have this a horrible feelin' that we've lost out on this. I hate to admit that one, stinkin' saddlebum got the better of us but it sure looks that way. We don't even have any horses now. We had him pinned down, now he's got us pinned down. He could pick us off any time he wants to.'

'Then we must get back to Cottonwood and tell the sheriff,' said the Indian. 'He will call out the army. Your Mr McNally might be good, but even he could not hope to defeat the army.'

'It's a long walk back to Cottonwood,' Edwards pointed out.

'There is one horse,' said the Indian. 'The one belonging to McNally. It is still in the village. I saw that it did not run off into the forest like the other ponies. It is our one chance.'

'Hell, so there is!' exclaimed Edwards, slapping his thigh. 'I'd forgotten all about that. Do you reckon we could get it without him seein' us?'

'It's the only option we have,' said Steve, one of Edwards' men. 'Like you, I reckon we don't stand much chance out here on our own against someone like McNally. I'm all for gettin' his horse an' one of us ridin' back to Cottonwood. The rest of us will probably be able to hold him off until somebody gets here.'

'I do not understand,' said one of the other Indian policemen. 'You talk as though this man was some kind of spirit. Is he not just a man of flesh and blood like any other man? Will he not die if he is shot through the heart?'

'You don't know McNally,' said Edwards. 'Sure, if you stick him he'll bleed just like any other man, the problem is stickin' him.'

'But there are six of us,' said the Indian policeman. 'No man can hold out against six guns.'

'Not if all six of us had the draw on him,' admitted Edwards. 'We don't have the drop on him though an' I don't reckon we're likely to either. OK, I agree the best chance is to get his horse an' one of us go back to Cottonwood. We'll all get back to the village. I reckon we can hold him off providin' we all stick together. Who's goin' to try an' get through?'

'I'll go,' volunteered Steve.

'OK,' agreed Edwards. 'Just remember, you're takin' a chance. He could be anywhere in the forest an' it ain't easy goin'. Remember we had to lead our horses some of the way.'

'Well we can't stay here for ever,' said Steve. 'I guess someone has to try an' it might as well be me.'

'OK, let's go,' commanded Edwards.

Very slowly and very cautiously they made their way back to the clearing and what was left of the village. At first they remained amongst the trees looking and listening, uncertain whether Brogan was also somewhere amongst the trees. Eventually Edwards indicated that they should move into the clearing. They were all rather surprised when they were not challenged. Brogan's horse was still saddled and Steve lost no time in leading the animal out of the crude paddock even though she plainly objected.

'I'd say this horse was about ready for the knackerman,' grunted Steve as he mounted. 'I hope she lasts the journey, she looks like a good run will bust her heart.'

'Then you'd better make sure she does make it,'

said Edwards. 'The important thing is to get there, you just remember that.'

The horse was certainly very old, even Brogan had no idea just how old she was, but in the many years she and Brogan had been together, she had never been ridden by anyone else and it seemed that she did not take too kindly to the idea on this occasion.

For a few moments she stubbornly refused to move as Steve dug in his heels and urged her forward. When one of the Indian policemen thought he would help by slapping her hard on her rump, she suddenly lashed out with her hind legs and caught the man full in the stomach, at the same time neighing loudly. The man, although in obvious pain, was little more than badly winded. Quite suddenly and with another loud neigh, she shot off towards the forest with Steve clinging on grimly. In a matter of seconds both horse and rider were lost amongst the trees.

Jimmy Two Rivers looked at Brogan when they heard the neighing of the horse. Brogan's reaction was simply to smile and nod his head.

'It's goin' to take a good horseman to get the better of her,' he said. 'She might be old but she's got a mind of her own. Come on, I reckon they won't get very far.'

Not worrying too much about being heard, Brogan led the three Indians at a run through the forest away from the village. It appeared that at least he knew where they were going even if the Indians did not. They reached the narrow trail just in time to see the horse galloping towards them with Steve doing his best to control her. Jimmy Two Rivers raised his rifle and was about to shoot when Brogan stopped him and stepped out into the path of the horse.

On seeing Brogan, the horse dug her front legs into the earth and stopped suddenly. Steve stood no chance and hurtled over the horse's head, landing, very hard, head first on the ground. Brogan went forward and steadied the animal and glanced down at the body.

'I'd say he broke his neck,' he said. One of the Indians bent down and examined the body and spoke to Two Rivers.

'As you say, his neck is broken,' confirmed Two Rivers. 'It would seem that you are a man of many talents,' he continued. 'Never before have I seen a horse do anything like that.'

'That's 'cos you ain't never come across a horse like her before,' said Brogan with a broad smile as he patted her neck. 'Well done, old girl. I was wonderin' how I was goin' to get you back.'

'Now there are only five of them,' said Two Rivers. 'Soon they will be none. I think the time has come to strike against them.'

'Wait here while I hide her somewhere. I don't want anyone tryin' to ride her again an' I want her where I can get to her if I need to,' said Brogan. He led the horse up a small slope and disappeared from view.

Jimmy Two Rivers spoke to his companions who nodded eagerly and they too disappeared, this time along the track towards the village. They soon reached the clearing where they saw the five remaining men in the process of erecting some timbers and rocks to make cover for themselves. The watching Indians did not think much of it when two of the Indian policemen suddenly stopped working, looked around, spoke briefly to Edwards; and disappeared into the forest. They assumed they had gone to find more timbers.

It appeared that being presented with what seemed easy targets was too much for one of the Indians with Two Rivers and he suddenly opened fire. He was plainly not used to the rifle he was holding and his shot was off target. There was little else that Two Rivers and the other Indian could do but also to open fire. They did not hear the shots behind them until it was too late....

'Bloody fools!' grated Brogan as he raced back to where he had left Two Rivers. 'Bloody stupid fools. I told 'em not do anythin'.' He was racing along the track in the direction of the shooting before he really had time to think. The shooting stopped before he reached the clearing and he held back, fearing the worst. His caution proved justified.

'Three Lakotas,' he heard a voice shout. 'We have killed two of them but one has escaped. I think he is injured.'

'Not McNally?' he heard Edwards ask.

'No, he was not one of them,' said the voice. 'He must have heard the shooting, perhaps he will come to investigate.'

'I heard!' called Brogan, unable to resist. 'Sorry to disappoint you, Edwards.'

'I didn't really think it'd be you,' called Edwards. 'It wasn't your style.'

'What is my style?' asked Brogan. 'I can adapt to almost anythin'.'

'Then maybe you'd better start adaptin' to tryin' to outshoot a whole regiment of soldiers,' said Edwards, laughing. 'Steve rode out on your horse to tell them in Cottonwood.'

'You mean he *tried* to ride to Cottonwood,' called Brogan. 'It must've been obvious that he was out of control on my horse. Right now he's lyin' no more'n four hundred yards away with a broken neck an' I've got my horse back. I was hopin' to get her back, we've been together a long time.'

'Damn you, McNally!' grated Edwards. 'You must have the devil on your side.'

'I prefer to work alone,' called Brogan. 'One of those three who just shot at you was Jimmy Two Rivers, maybe you'd better check if he wasn't the one who got away.'

'You knew about them?'

'Sure,' said Brogan. 'Stupid fools. I told 'em not to do anythin' like that but they wouldn't listen. Anyhow, it means I'm on my own now an' that's the way I like it. You're down to five now. The odds are gettin' better all the time an' time is somethin' I've got plenty of.'

Brogan moved quickly and quietly away, knowing that it was more than likely that one of the Indian policemen had pinpointed his position by then. He was in no hurry to do anything, in fact he was quite enjoying himself.

He slowly circled the clearing until he found somewhere which gave him plenty of cover and a good view. He could see four of the men – the two remaining white men and two of the Indian policemen – reinforcing their position and ruled out an attack on them. He assumed that they had a good supply of ammunition and he knew that there was a good supply of water and food in the remains of the village, so a lone assault would achieve virtually nothing. He would sit and wait for the opportunity to take them out one at a time.

He had just settled himself when he became aware of heavy breathing close by and slowly he parted a nearby bush. The blood-spattered face of Jimmy Two Rivers stared back at him, terror in his eyes. The look of terror changed to relief when he recognized Brogan.

'We . . . we thought we could help,' croaked Two Rivers. 'I am sorry, we did not listen to you. . . .'

'Nobody ever listens to a saddlebum,' muttered Brogan. 'Maybe you'll listen next time – if there is a next time. Where are you hurt?'

Two Rivers weakly raised his arm away from his stomach to reveal a large wound in his side and pointed to his leg where there was another wound. Brogan examined the hole in his side.

'I've seen worse,' he pronounced. 'You've lost a lot of blood but at least your guts seem to be intact. Looks like the bullet passed straight through.' He looked at the wound in his thigh and felt the leg. 'I reckon it's busted the bone. OK,' he sighed, sitting back. 'I guess that puts you out of action but at least you're still alive which is more than can be said for your friends.'

'I am sorry, it was very foolish, but I had to show you that we are able to look after ourselves,' said Two Rivers.

'Yeh, an' you just showed me!' said Brogan sarcastically. 'The question is what do I do with you now? I could leave you here an' ride off I suppose. If I had any sense that's exactly what I would do.'

'My people,' croaked Two Rivers. 'Some of them will have gone to some caves. I will try to get to them. There is nothing else you can do, Mr McNally. You have done your best but it was not good enough. I thank you all the same.'

'Now that's gratitude for you,' said Brogan. 'I'll have you know, my young buck, that Brogan McNally don't settle for second best. How far are these caves from here and which way?'

'To the north,' replied Two Rivers. 'Two hours at the most.'

'Two hours for a man what ain't draggin' a busted leg you mean,' said Brogan. 'OK, I'll get you there. You just hang on here till I get back an' don't go gettin' any ideas about actin' on your own.'

'I do not have a gun,' said Two Rivers with a rueful smile. 'Do not worry, my friend, I shall be here when you return this time.'

'Well if you ain't I sure ain't goin' lookin' for you,' said Brogan. 'You just pull that bush over you an' act like you was dead. You got that?' Two Rivers nodded weakly. 'I'll go get my horse.'

Brogan checked on the activity in the clearing and saw that there were still only two white men and two Indians. The absence of the third Indian policeman worried him somewhat For a few moments he sat and listened but could hear nothing other than the breathing of Jimmy Two Rivers and sounds made by the men in the clearing. Rather reluctantly he slowly made his way back to where he had left his horse.

His caution and slow pace suddenly disappeared as the unmistakable snorting of his horse broke the silence. He arrived at where he had tethered his horse just in time to see the missing Indian policeman raise his rifle at the horse's head.

'No you don't,' snarled Brogan, rifle in hand. 'That ain't no way to treat an old lady like her.' The Indian turned too late. Brogan's rifle spat its message of death and the Indian fell, wide-eyed but sightless, to the ground.

Without really thinking, Brogan took the dead man's guns and gunbelt and also the guns and gunbelt the man had apparently recovered from the body of Steve. He patted his horse and apologized for leaving her and promised that he would not do so again.

'That leaves four of you,' he called as he led his horse through the forest. 'Which one of you wants to be next?'

'You'll be next, McNally,' came the answer. 'I can promise you that.'

'I'd say you was a man what never keeps promises,' called Brogan with a derisory laugh.

NINE

Brogan made his way back and found that Two Rivers appeared much weaker than before. Blood was flowing quite freely from the wound in his side. Even though the wound itself did not appear to be too serious, the Indian was obviously losing a great deal of blood. He tore some cloth from Two Rivers' few clothes and tried to staunch the flow as best he could. The leg he could do nothing about. He looked at Two Rivers and then at his horse and sighed heavily.

'This is goin' to hurt,' he whispered. 'I have to get you on my horse an' the only way is for me to lift you.'

'As you said before, my friend,' said Two Rivers, smiling weakly. 'At least I am still alive. Do not be afraid of hurting me.'

'I won't,' said Brogan, slipping his arms under Two Rivers' body. 'Just make sure you don't shout out. Right now the last thing we want is them knowin' where we are. Do you want a stick to bite on while I lift you?'

'I will not shout, my friend,' assured Two Rivers. 'An Indian warrior does not admit to pain.'

'Well I can assure you this *is* goin' to hurt,' said Brogan.

He lifted the surprisingly light body as slowly and as evenly as he could and for a moment it seemed that Two Rivers was going to cry out. However, he clenched his teeth and held on to Brogan as tightly as he could but apart from a slight groan did not cry out.

Lifting the Indian was the first and easiest part. The next problem was to get him astride the horse. He was quite amazed when Two Rivers did not scream out in pain as he had to force the uninjured leg across the back of his horse while holding the broken leg. He heard and felt a distinct crack as the bone in his already broken leg moved once again under the strain. Two Rivers clamped his fist into his mouth but still did not cry out.

'Reckon you can keep it straight?' whispered Brogan as he pushed the Indian into an upright position. 'It's goin' to be a long ride an' from what I've seen it ain't too easy goin'.'

'If you can make it, so can I,' croaked Two Rivers, swaying unsteadily.

Brogan rummaged in one of his saddle-bags and took out a length of rope which he passed round Two Rivers' back before he too mounted, this time in the saddle. He then tied the rope tightly round himself and Two Rivers.

'That's the best I can do,' he said. 'Now hold tight. North you said?' Two Rivers grunted weakly which Brogan took to mean 'yes'. 'Now I'm only guessin' since I can't see the sun, but I'd say north was that way . . .' He pointed briefly. 'Now don't go passin' out on me or anythin' like that, I need you to direct me to these caves.'

'Do not worry, my friend,' croaked Two Rivers. 'I will guide you. I must ask why you do not leave me? You have your horse and they do not have theirs, it would be easy for you to ride away and save yourself.'

'I ask myself that very same question,' admitted Brogan. 'Let's just say I started this so I feel I have to finish it.'

'There are very few white men who think as you do,' said Two Rivers. 'I think you are a man of honour.'

'More like pure bloody-mindedness,' muttered Brogan 'Now shut up until I ask you which way to go.'

'Soon you will be able to see two mountains,' said Two Rivers. 'All you have to do is ride towards them. I still do not understand. Surely it would be better for you to kill these men before you take me to the caves? It is possible that they will not be here when you return.'

'Who said anythin' about comin' back?' asked Brogan. 'I'll have to think about that later.'

It was about half an hour later, half an hour of very slow going, when, as they negotiated a somewhat steep slope on which there were fewer trees, he saw the two mountains ahead of him. He guessed that they were about ten miles away and immediately questioned the Indian's statement that it would take about two hours to reach the caves.

'That is because the caves are not among those mountains,' said Two Rivers when questioned. 'All you have to do is keep them in sight. I will. tell you when we are near the caves.'

For another hour, during which he lost sight of

the mountains several times, they negotiated rather less dense forest. They eventually came across a river and Brogan, thinking that Two Rivers had passed out, was just about to cross when the Indian spoke.

'Do not cross,' he croaked. 'Turn to the right and follow the river until I tell you. We are almost there.'

'And you are sure your people will have come here?' queried Brogan.

'Most of them will be here,' said Two Rivers. 'It had been agreed that we should come here if we had to. They are easy to defend.'

'Even against soldiers?' asked Brogan.

'There are secret ways we can use if we need to,' said Two Rivers. 'If that happens we can easily escape.'

Ten minutes later Two Rivers nudged Brogan and pointed towards a high ridge and in another ten minutes he found himself at the base of a large scree. Suddenly he was aware that he was surrounded and men were rushing forward to help Two Rivers off the horse. It appeared that they had been expecting the injured man as they already had a crude stretcher prepared. For the first time, as they lifted him off the horse, Two Rivers allowed himself the luxury of a cry of pain.

'Welcome,' said one of the older men. 'We had not thought to see you or Two Rivers again.'

'He nearly didn't make it,' said Brogan. 'He's hurt bad an' there's nothin' I can do for him. It's a pity you don't have a doctor. I guess you have your medicine man though. It looks like you was expectin' us. I normally sense when I'm bein' watched but then it ain't often I come across Indians.'

'You were seen long before you reached us,' said

the old man. 'There are what you call look-outs posted all around. It is impossible for anyone to reach us without being seen. Do not worry, all will be well. Now, you must be hungry. The women have food prepared. You will be safe here.'

'It ain't me I'm bothered about,' said Brogan. 'Still, I have to admit that it looks like you could hold out here for a long time. Are those the caves at the top of that loose rock?'

'You do not have to climb up there,' said the old man. 'Come, we will follow the others.'

They followed an almost circular route around some large boulders, climbing all the time and finally traversing a very narrow path with a fifty-foot sheer drop. They came out on to a fairly wide ledge off which were at least five caves. Two Rivers was taken into the first and Brogan was led to the second cave. The smell of roasting meat reminded Brogan that he was very hungry. He had lost track of the last time he had eaten. Too much had been happening for him to bother about such things.

The caves were very deceptive. The entrances were quite low but once inside, although very gloomy, Brogan could see that after about twenty or so yards, this particular cave suddenly increased in height and width quite dramatically. In fact he was unable to see the roof. All around family groups were in the process of cooking or engaged in other quite normal chores. It seemed that the other caves also came out into this one large chamber.

From seemingly nowhere, water and some fodder were provided for his horse and a large platter of roast meat, which he guessed was deer, and some unknown vegetables was given to him. After he had eaten the old man approached him again.

'Two Rivers will be well,' he assured. 'He has lost much blood but we have special herbs and plants which will replace the lost blood. You are not injured?' Brogan shook his head. 'That is good,' continued the old man. 'We would not like you to be injured on our behalf. The men who attacked, are they all dead?'

'Four of 'em are,' said Brogan. 'Two white men and two of the policemen.'

'Unfortunately there will be much trouble when it is known,' said the old man. 'For a white man to kill an Indian is nothing. A white man would be in more trouble if he were to refuse to pay a gambling debt than if he killed an Indian. But for an Indian to kill a white man is to bring down the full weight of the army upon them and the army will kill every Indian they find.' He sighed heavily. 'That is the way of things, I fear. I sometimes think that the white man will not rest until every Indian has been killed.'

'It sure looks that way in California,' admitted Brogan. 'It don't seem quite so bad in most other places. Maybe you should all leave California.'

'These have been our lands since time began,' said the old man. 'No matter what the white man may do to us our spirits would never rest in peace in any other land. Our dead are brought here. They are laid far into the cave so you will not see any bodies.'

'I guess that's where I have the advantage,' said Brogan. 'I ain't never been tied to any one place. I come an' go as I please so, when my time comes, it don't matter that much where I die. As far as I'm concerned when I've done with this old body it might as well be used to feed the buzzards. I sure won't notice what happens to it.'

'You do not have what the white man calls a god?'

'I've thought about it from time to time,' admitted Brogan, 'an' it seems to me that if there is such a thing it don't really matter where I live or die. No, I don't really believe in such things.'

'Then there is nothing else to be said,' said the old man. 'Such thinking certainly makes life much easier. Now, what will you do? You are quite welcome to remain among us as long as you wish, but I sense that you not stay long. You are what is known as a drifter, are you not?' Brogan nodded. 'Then you will not be happy in one place for too long. This I understand. The Lakota too were once free to roam these lands but that is all gone now. We are little more than prisoners in our own lands. You are welcome to stay as long as you may please.'

'Thanks,' said Brogan. 'I reckon I'll stay tonight but, much as I would like to, I can't hang about, there are things still to be done. Tomorrow I must be on my way. I can't help worryin' about what will happen to you though. Those men will not remain where they are for much longer and then they will go back to Cottonwood and tell the sheriff what has happened. At least they'll give their version of what happened. I doubt if they will tell the truth. It's a certain fact that the army will be sent up here to hunt you down an' no matter what escape routes you have, they will find you an' kill you.'

The old man sighed heavily. 'Yes, I fear that you are right. But, that has not happened yet. Perhaps, if the Great Spirit is willing, it never will.'

'I wouldn't rely on it,' warned Brogan.

Later, Brogan was taken to see Jimmy Two Rivers who certainly looked a lot better than he had before. The wound in his side had been stitched – somewhat crudely Brogan thought – but the leg had been very expertly straightened and was in a splint.

'I guess you won't be leadin' your people against the white man for quite some time,' he said to Two Rivers. 'Maybe you'd be better off usin' your influence to get your people to somewhere safer.'

'These caves are safe,' said Two Rivers. 'Even the army would have difficulty in getting up here.'

'Difficult, yes,' agreed Brogan. 'Impossible, no. What I don't quite understand is if these caves are so safe, why don't you live here all the time?'

'Because they are a sacred place,' explained Two Rivers, 'Our dead are buried here. These caves are the homes of our ancestors. It is permissible to use them as we do now, as a place of refuge, but if we stay here too long we will become what we call the living dead. The spirits of our ancestors will help us only for a certain time until the danger has passed. They do not like to be disturbed when there is no need. If we remain beyond that time they will take our souls, leaving only the body which slowly rots. This is the fate of the living dead.'

'Living dead?' asked Brogan.

'If you are unfortunate enough to set your eyes upon them you will know,' said Two Rivers. 'Have you not been warned?'

'Nobody's said a thing,' said Brogan.

'Then be warned,' said Two Rivers, gravely. 'Do not go to the two caves furthest away from here. That is where the living dead are to be found.'

'You mean there are actually some of 'em here – now?'

'They are here,' assured Two Rivers. 'We never see them but we leave food for them. It is forbidden to look upon them. To do so is to be condemned to be one of them. We are safe enough in these caves for the moment. They do not come here, they are forbidden to do so.'

'And how long have you got before your ancestors take away your spirits?'

'That we do not know,' admitted Two Rivers, 'but there will be signs. What will you do now, my friend?'

'Whatever I decide, I'll leave here in the mornin',' said Brogan. 'I ain't decided what I'm goin' to do next. I'll have to think about it.'

'As I see it,' said Two Rivers, 'you have little choice but to leave and save yourself. You have done all you can to help us and my people know this. It is much more than any other white man would have done for us and we thank you. Whatever you decide, may the Great Spirit guide you.'

'I don't know about that,' said Brogan. 'I ain't never noticed him helpin' me before an' I don't think he's likely to be too concerned about an old saddlebum like me what don't even believe in him.'

'Nobody knows the ways of the Great Spirit,' said Two Rivers. 'He is all around even when you do not think so. You have been through many dangers and yet you are still here, is that not so?' Brogan nodded. 'That is the way the Great Spirit works.'

'That's too deep for me,' said Brogan. 'I'd rather rely on my own senses, my horse an' my guns.'

Brogan left Two Rivers and wandered out of the cave and stood looking across a wooded valley for some time. He was actually wondering what to do next when he idly glanced in the direction of the two forbidden caves. He had dismissed the story of the living dead as nothing but Indian folklore but a very slight movement just inside the end cave made him curious.

He seemed to be alone and took the opportunity to slowly wander towards the two caves. He had no wish to offend the beliefs and ways of the Indians but another slight movement made him determined to see who or what was inside the cave. The one thing of which he was quite certain was that if there were people in there, they were certainly not living dead.

He soon reached the caves and listened for a few moments. His keen sense of hearing picked up very definite sounds and his sense of smell detected a very strange odour. He had the feeling that he had come across the smell at least once before in the past but he could not recall where or when.

Making sure that nobody saw him, he slipped into the gloom, his gun in hand just in case there was any trouble. As he entered there were sudden sounds of several people or possibly animals scuttling away from him. He could just make out several cowering forms heading towards the back of the cave.

'You must not come any further!' a voice suddenly croaked at him. 'You must leave, white man. To look upon us is to look upon death.'

Brogan could just make out a shape huddled against the side of the cave apparently covered in rags and he stepped forward. The obviously human form hissed and cowered but that did not deter Brogan. He reached forward and pulled the rags off where he assumed the face would be. What he saw in the light from the entrance to the cave made him step back slightly but it did not horrify him. He had seen exactly the same thing twice before in his life and immediately recognized it. He also remembered where and when he had come across the smell.

'You're a leper,' he said.

'We are the living dead,' hissed the disfigured face.

'I guess some folk would agree with you,' said Brogan. 'I've seen it before. Last time was down in Mexico.'

'You have seen such a thing before?' croaked the face. 'You have seen yet you are still not one of us?'

'I've seen it before,' said Brogan, 'an' no, I still ain't one of you.'

'Then leave us before it is too late,' said the face. 'Go, leave us to die.'

'OK,' agreed Brogan. 'I guess there ain't nothin' I can do. I ain't sure if there's anythin' anyone can do either but I ain't no doctor.' The form suddenly scuttled away leaving Brogan with a few unanswered question.

He returned to the daylight and made his way back to the other caves. At least he now understood just why the Indians were not able or too afraid to spend too much time in the caves. It was always possible that they too would succumb to the flesh-eating disease.

'You have seen the living dead,' said the old man as Brogan entered the cave. 'I should have warned you.'

'I've seen a leper,' said Brogan. 'He was livin' but

he sure wasn't dead. There are such people in other places and for the most part they are looked after, usually by religious men. It is possible to help them, you know. What's wrong with them ain't nothin' at all do with your ancestors. They have a terrible disease an' they need help, not shuttin' away from the world. That's the way people who do not understand behave.'

'Yes, this much I know,' said the old man. 'But who is there who would want to help such people? The white man's cure would be to kill them all. The white man seems determined to kill even healthy Indians, so they would certainly not change their minds for those of my people so terribly afflicted.'

'Yeh, probably you're right,' agreed Brogan. 'How many of them are there?'

'Perhaps twenty of them,' replied the old man. 'We do not really know. We do our best to see that they are fed but there is little else we can do for them.'

'Or would want to do for them, I suspect,' said Brogan. 'OK, it ain't my problem I guess.'

'No, it is not your problem,' said the old man.

Brogan spent most of the remaining daylight hours sitting outside the caves considering what to do next. There was no doubt in his mind that if Carl Edwards and the remaining men were to get back to Cottonwood, the army would be called out. If that happened he did not hold out much hope for the future of the healthy Indians and even less hope for those afflicted with leprosy.

Word had obviously spread that Brogan had seen the so-called living dead and it was very noticeable that apart from the old man, everyone else did their best to avoid him. They obviously feared that he had

Squaw Hunters

been contaminated and did not want to take the risk of him passing on the disease. It did not bother him particularly, in fact he preferred to be left alone.

Shortly after dark, more food was brought for him but the woman who brought it would not come too close, placing it on the ground a few yards from him and then quickly retreating. He smiled as he tried to pick up what he thought was a platter only to discover that it was in fact a large leaf. The woman was obviously taking no chances of the disease being spread through his contact with one of their wooden platters. He ate the food provided and, with several of them watching, deliberately threw the soiled leaf over the edge of the cliff.

Brogan suddenly became aware of the old man walking towards him and the look on the man's face told him that all was not well. He wondered if something had happened to Jimmy Two Rivers. The fact that Brogan had been close to the lepers did not appear to bother the old man too much.

'Men come,' said the old man. 'There are five of them, three white men and two Indian policemen. They can only be the men who attacked our village. They must have recovered their horses and have followed you here.'

'Five!' exclaimed Brogan. 'That's impossible. I know for certain there was only eight of 'em an' that four of 'em have been killed. Are you sure there's five of 'em? If there are five, where did the other one come from?'

'I am sure,' replied the old man. 'They have followed you here knowing that you would lead them to us. Now they will return and tell the army where we are.'

'Where are they now?' asked Brogan.

'They make camp alongside the river,' said the old man.

'Well, if you know where they are,' said Brogan, 'it'd be a simple matter to send some men out to kill them.'

'I have talked of this with Two Rivers and he agrees with you,' said the old man. 'However, it has so far proved impossible to find any men who are willing to go and kill them. We no longer have any guns, they were all lost when our village was attacked. Spears and bows will be useless against them. You are the only man with guns. You are also the only man here who really knows how to use modern guns properly.'

'So you want me to finish the job off?' said Brogan. 'I suppose that's what I intended doin' anyway. Five of 'em though. Where the hell did the fifth man come from? OK, I'll go and make sure they are the men who attacked the village. It is possible that it might not be them and just some strangers passin' through.'

'They are the same men,' said the old man. 'We are certain of that. The two policemen were already known to us.'

'OK, I'll go see,' said Brogan. 'I ain't promisin' nothin' though.'

The old man directed Brogan to where the men were camped, which was not too far away, so he left his horse. Taking his rifle, he slowly made his way down into the valley.

It was obvious that the men were not too concerned about being seen. They probably knew that they already had been and made no attempt to hide their presence. Brogan managed to get within about thirty yards of them without arousing their suspicions and he saw, in the glow from the fire, that there were indeed five of them. Four of them he recognized straight away, but the fifth had his back towards him and it was some time before he saw who he was.

'Deputy!' he said to himself. 'Now just what the hell are you doin' here?'

The fifth man was indeed the deputy who had escorted him out of Cottonwood. His presence threw a very different light on what he should do next.

TEN

Had it not been for the presence of the deputy, Brogan might well have tried to kill the other four and thought no more about it. However, he was not prepared to kill the deputy in cold blood. As far as he was concerned that *would* amount to murder and, while his reasons for killing some men had come questionably close to murder, he had always been able to justify his actions. At that moment he could think of no way to justifying the killing of the deputy and his own conscience would not allow him to resort to killing for no reason. He thought about the problem for a while and eventually made his way back to the caves.

'I just wish I knew what he was doin' here,' he said to Two Rivers and the old man. 'I don't think there's anyone else, at least not yet. It could be that the army is on the way but I don't think so. That's one of the things I need to find out for certain before I do anythin' else.'

'I understand your hesitation, my friend,' said Two Rivers. 'To kill men such as Edwards is one thing as far as you are concerned but to kill a white lawman is another. For us it does not matter who the white man is, they will hunt us and kill us if we should kill *any* white man. I can but suggest that you take your horse and make good your escape. You have done all you can for us, we must now put our trust in the Great Spirit.'

'I said before, I'd rather put my trust in my guns,' said Brogan. 'There's only five of 'em an' you could probably deal with 'em even if you are armed only with spears an' bows an' arrows. The thing is if the deputy is here, the sheriff probably knows where he is an' when he doesn't get back he'll send out the army for sure, even if he hasn't done so already. Somehow I don't think the army is involved just yet, at least I hope not.'

'The forest is very large,' said the old man. 'We will be able to avoid them.'

'For how long?' asked Brogan. 'I think the best thing I can do is talk to the deputy an' find out why he's here. It just strikes me as peculiar that he should take the chance of comin' out here by himself.'

'And how will you talk to the deputy?' asked Two Rivers. 'The others could easily kill you and the very fact that you have already taken up arms against them would be justification enough.'

'Then I have to get him on his own,' said Brogan.

It was just after midnight when Brogan slipped silently from the caves and made his way back to where the men were camped. It seemed that they were confident enough not to post a look-out and the fire had been allowed to die down. Brogan got as close as he reasonably could and checked that there were five of them sleeping. His initial problem was making out which was the deputy. To wake the wrong man might well have proved disastrous.

At first it was quite impossible to tell which of the three white men was the deputy. The two Indian policemen were fairly easy to identify as they slept well apart from the others. His problem was eventually solved when one of the forms turned over and Brogan caught the flash of a metal badge of office. Luckily for him the deputy was the one furthest from the fire.

'Not a sound!' whispered Brogan as he clamped his hand across the deputy's mouth. The deputy looked up to see a gun also pointed at his head. 'I want to talk to you, Deputy,' he continued, his head very close to the deputy's ear. 'Don't think I won't kill you, I don't stand to lose much if I do. Now get up an' follow me.'

Surprisingly, as far as Brogan was concerned, the deputy made no attempt to struggle nor to alert his companions and obediently followed Brogan into the bushes. When they were far enough away, Brogan placed his finger against his lips to indicate silence while he listened. Eventually he was satisfied.

'What's this all about, McNally?' whispered the deputy. 'Carl Edwards told me you murdered three of his men and two of the policemen. If that is the case then I have to arrest you but I think there must be more to it than that.'

'There's a hell of a lot more to it,' said Brogan. 'Sure, I killed three of 'em back at the village but it was a case of them or me. The other one, the one they call Steve, fell off my horse an' broke his neck. What I want to know is what the hell you're doin' out here? Does the sheriff know you're here?'

'He does,' replied the deputy. 'After I left you at Hog Back Ridge, I met Carl Edwards and his men and they didn't hide the fact that they were out to get you. I went back to Cottonwood and told Max Ford. I expected him to do something about it but all he said was that it was your tough luck. I told Mary, his daughter, an' I've got to admit that it was her idea that I come out here and try to warn you and warn the Indians about the policemen. So here I am.'

'Unfortunately you are a bit late,' said Brogan. 'You must have found where I hid their horses.'

'One of the Indians found them,' said the deputy. 'Following you was easy enough. At least it was for the Indians.'

'So now you know where they're hidin',' said Brogan.

'One of the policemen remembered hearing about the caves,' said the deputy.

'Do they know what's in there?'

'In there?' asked the deputy. 'What is there to know? He said something about it being a Lakota burial site, that's all.'

'Among other things,' said Brogan, not enlightening the deputy. 'OK, that explains your reason for bein' here. What's your next move?'

'I've tried talking them all out of it,' said the deputy. 'The two policemen are quite adamant that they intend to get Jimmy Two Rivers. There"s a reward out on him and they intend to collect it and since they were sent out by the sheriff there's not a lot I can do about it. It seems you really have got to Carl Edwards and he intends to kill you.'

'You could arrest him for murder if he does,' said Brogan.

'Not a chance,' replied the deputy. 'You killed at least two white men and there isn't a jury in the whole of California which would convict him. He says you killed the first man out at some Indian farm.'

'They were going to rape and probably kill two Indian women,' said Brogan. 'I couldn't let 'em do that. I hadn't intended to kill him, he just moved at the wrong time.'

'Unfortunately,' sighed the deputy, 'raping or even killing Indian women is not an offence in California. At least that is effectively the case since no Indian can give evidence either for or against a white man.'

'I gathered as much,' said Brogan. 'I guess this means that they intend to try an' get into the caves an' kill as many as they can.'

'That's about the size of it,' admitted the deputy. 'Again, unfortunately, they won't be breaking any laws. There's a wanted man up there and if anyone else dies while they are trying to arrest him it's just hard luck.'

'I thought so,' said Brogan. 'There's a lot of people up there, there is a chance they might come off worse.'

'I don't think so and neither do you,' said the deputy. 'They know for certain that Two Rivers was injured. We found traces of blood along the trail here. Is he hurt bad?'

'Bad enough,' admitted Brogan.

'They also think, and I agree with them, that the Indians up there don't have any guns worth speaking of,' continued the deputy. 'We collected a whole lot of them back at the village. I'd say you were the only man up there who has guns.'

'And I know how to use them,' said Brogan. 'You just remember that. If I was you I'd keep well away from things. It wouldn't be the first time I've taken on four or even more men an' come out on top.'

'That, I can well believe,' said the deputy. 'Right now though I'd say your best chance was to get the hell out of it. I shouldn't say this but I'll make sure you can get well away. If you head for the border there shouldn't be no more bother.'

'And leave the Indians to be slaughtered? No chance,' said Brogan. 'Maybe they ain't got no rights as far as California law is concerned, but in my eyes they're human an' that means they got rights just like any other human. No, Deputy, I guess you've just solved a problem for me.'

'And created another,' said the deputy.

'And created another,' admitted Brogan. 'What the hell though, there ain't nobody gives a damn what happens to an old saddlebum. let alone some Indians so I might as well go down fightin'.'

'It's a pity,' said the deputy. 'I kinda like you, McNally. Look at it this way. Maybe there is a chance you will come out on top, but in the long run it won't make a blind bit of difference to how things are in California or anywhere else. Indians will still be hunted, their women will still be raped by men like Carl Edwards. Their children will still be sold into apprenticeships and vagrant Indians will still be forced into four months' indentured service. You might be able to get rid of one lot of so-called squaw hunters but another lot will simply take their place. That, unfortunately, is the way of things in California.'

'Unfortunately,' agreed Brogan. 'But at least I will have the satisfaction of having done my best. That's the way things are with me.'

'They know you are with the Indians,' said the deputy. 'That's reason enough in most folks' eyes. Indian-lovers are not popular.'

'Is that how you see it?' asked Brogan.

'No, but then most folk don't know you like I do,' replied the deputy. 'I haven't known you long but long enough to appreciate how your mind works. Now, you'd better decide what you're goin' to do next. They're all set on wipin' out the Indians in those caves an' you along with them an' there ain't a damned thing I can do about it.'

'Or would want to?'

'That ain't what I said, McNally,' said the deputy. 'Unfortunately my feelin's don't come into it.'

'OK, Deputy,' said Brogan. 'At least I know where I stand. Just take my advice an' keep out of it. I'd hate to have to kill you but I will if necessary.' Brogan did not give the deputy a chance to reply as he suddenly disappeared among the bushes.

'It has been decided,' said the old man. 'We will leave these caves and take to the forest. We will leave now, while it is still dark.'

'And what about the ones you call the living dead?' asked Brogan.

The old man looked down at the ground and slowly shook his head. 'There is nothing we can do for them. They cannot come with us and it is forbidden for any of my people to have contact with them.'

'So you just leave 'em to be slaughtered?' said Brogan.

'It is not a decision which is mine alone,' said the old man. 'The council of elders has ruled and we are bound to obey.' He looked up at Brogan and for the first time Brogan saw a tear in the corner of the old man's eye. 'It is not a decision which I take lightly. You see, my own wife and my son are among the living dead. They were taken two summers ago. They will all die soon, there is nothing we can do about that. Perhaps this is the Great Spirit's way of ending their torment.'

'But it ain't mine!' snarled Brogan, becoming very angry for one of the few occasions in his life. 'OK, get the hell out of here, all of you. Maybe bein' out in the forest is the only chance you have. Just remember this though. Neither your wife nor your son asked for what they've got. No matter what you believe it's a disease they have, it has nothin' to do with your so-called Great Spirit. Go ahead, scuttle out of these caves like a bunch of stinkin' rats, I'm stayin' to see what I can do to help.'

The old man turned and looked into the darkness of the cave. 'Already my people are leaving,' he said. 'Two Rivers did not want to leave you but he is too badly injured to be of any help. In a few minutes we shall be on our own.'

'We?' queried Brogan.

The old man sighed. 'I have decided to defy the ruling of the elders. My wife and son are here. There is no reason for me to join the others. I am staying. If I must die then I wish it to be with my wife in my arms and my son at my side.'

'Glad to have you along,' Brogan said, a little hoarsely.

'Are you comin' with us, Deputy?' sneered Carl Edwards. 'You ain't been in these parts all that long an' I don't think you've ever been on an Indian hunt before. The experience will do you good. It's good fun too.'

'I don't share your idea of fun,' said the deputy. 'If I can't talk you out of it then I certainly do not want to be any part of it.'

'You've been payin' too much attention to Mary Ford,' said Edwards. 'Fine lookin' woman an' all that she might be, but I hear she's got some mighty strange ideas on just how Indians and coloureds should be treated. I don't think her pa agrees with her strange ideas either.'

'Just leave Mary out of this,' grated the deputy. 'Go ahead, do your damndest. Just remember, McNally's up there with 'em an' he's a very different proposition from a bunch of unarmed Indian squaws. He's got guns an' he knows haw to use 'em. You should know that more'n anyone else. I sure won't lose no sleep over you if he kills you.'

Carl Edwards touched his injured shoulder and grinned. 'Sure, I know that. I owe McNally an' I intend to deliver. OK, Deputy, you wait here like the yeller-bellied coward you are. I'll make sure Max an' Mary hear all about how brave you was.'

'You have to kill McNally first,' reminded the deputy.

At that moment, one of the Indian policemen appeared. 'I have found a way into the caves,' he said. 'They will be expecting us from the front. This way we can attack from behind. We shall have the advantage of having the light in front of us. They will not be able to see us coming from the dark side.'

'Good man,' said Edwards. 'OK – lead the way.

The deputy here is shit-scared of the dark so he won't be comin'.' He laughed coarsely.

The last of the Indians left the caves by a series of tunnels. Where they came out Brogan did not know and did not ask. As the final stragglers disappeared the old man appeared from the direction of the two caves where the lepers lived. Much to Brogan's surprise he carried a rifle. It might only have been a single-shot muzzle-loader but Brogan had to admit that even that would help.

There was about another hour until daybreak and Brogan wondered if Edwards would use the cover of darkness to make his way to the caves. He stationed himself in the entrance to the first cave which looked out on to the narrow path. He looked into the gloom listening for the slightest sound.

As the darkness began to lift, Brogan was suddenly aware of a number of ragged forms emerging from the far caves. There were about twenty of them, all armed, rather pathetically, with sharpened sticks as spears and one or two large knives. One of them slowly approached him but stopped a few yards short. Brogan guessed it was the man he had seen in the cave. The others slowly joined him and stood silently as if awaiting instructions. Eventually the leader of the group spoke.

'What would you have us do?' he asked. 'We do not have guns but we are all prepared to fight. To us, death would be a merciful release. We are doomed to die soon but the chance to die as warriors would mean that our lives are not completely wasted. We will meet our forefathers with honour.'

'I was wonderin' about you,' said Brogan. 'As far

as I'm concerned it don't matter what's wrong with you. I think the best thing you can do is go back to your caves and wait. As far as I know nobody else knows about you. You are used to the darkness and you probably know every rock inside these caves. When they come they'll search every cave an' when they do you can use the darkness to your advantage.'

'Would it not be better to stand here and fight?' asked the man.

'No,' said Brogan. 'I want you to be a surprise.' He looked down into the valley but could not detect any movement. 'I'm just surprised they haven't done anythin' yet. Now, if you do really want to help, do as I say.' Suddenly he looked back into the cave, listening intently. 'Are there any more of you back there?' he asked.

'We are all here,' said the man. 'Eleven men and nine women.'

'Then we've got company,' said Brogan. 'Is there any way they can get into the caves without comin' this way?'

'There are many ways,' said the man, 'but there is only one way they could use. There is a tunnel which leads up from the forest below us. It is narrow and difficult but it can be done.'

'Then I'd say they've found it,' said Brogan. 'Do as I say and get back to your caves. I reckon they're somewhere behind us.' The man spoke to his companions and they all returned to their caves. For a while silence descended as Brogan listened for the slightest sound. 'Did you know about the tunnel?' he eventually asked the old man.

'No, and I do not believe that anyone else did,' replied the old man.

Suddenly a shot ricocheted off a rock close to Brogan's head. Immediately both he and the old man dived for cover. A second shot showed that someone was at the entrance to the third cave. This was followed by another shot, again ricocheting off the rock close to them but this time it came from inside the first cave. Brogan cursed loudly but did not return fire. Apart from the man at the entrance to the third cave, who was well hidden, there was nothing to shoot at.

'It looks like they've all deserted you,' called the voice of Carl Edwards, echoing round the cave behind them. 'Can't say as I'm surprised, they're all cowards. I'm just surprised you're still here, McNally.'

'Some of 'em have gone,' called Brogan. 'There's a lot of ways out of here. They'll all be out in the forest by now. There's still enough left to deal with you though. I stayed because I wanted to make sure you never found 'em.'

'We'll find 'em,' said Edwards. 'If not us then the army will.'

'Are the army on the way?' asked Brogan.

'Not yet,' replied Edwards. 'You just lost your horse again, McNally. We've got it back here. You can try runnin' if you like, but there ain't nowhere for you to go. I think you're bluffin' about there still bein' some Indians here. We ain't seen no sign of 'em yet.'

'You will,' assured Brogan.

'In here!' came the sudden call from one of the policemen. 'They are hiding in the last two caves.'

'Then what are you waitin' for?' shouted Edwards. 'Kill 'em, kill 'em all! I'll keep McNally an' the other one pinned down. We can deal with them when the others are all dead.'

There was a burst of gunfire from the two caves but suddenly, and chillingly, there were two loud screams. One of the Indian policemen burst out of the cave, obviously terrified. In his haste he stumbled and was quite suddenly surrounded by several ragged figures who dragged him back inside. His cries of terror reverberated through the cave system.

'Christ! Let's get out of here!' called the other white man from somewhere inside the caves. 'Lepers, they're all bloody lepers! They've got the two policemen, there ain't nothin' we can do for them. Come on, Carl, let's get the hell out of it while we still can. I don't want to catch leprosy.'

'Lepers!' called Edwards. 'You knew about this, McNally. You knew about it an' just let us walk straight into it.'

'I knew,' laughed Brogan. 'I just wanted to keep it as a surprise.'

'They're behind us!' yelled the other man. Several shots echoed through the caves. 'Christ, Carl, They just keep on comin', they won't bloody well die.'

'They are known as the living dead,' called Brogan as the echoes died down. 'They don't die 'cos they're already dead.'

There followed a few minutes' comparative silence during which time Brogan and the old man managed to ease themselves into an upright position. The silence was suddenly broken as Carl Edwards and the other white man burst out of the adjoining cave.

The old man was the first to shoot and was very accurate. His shot sent the other white man sprawling into the dust. Carl Edwards had to hurdle the body as he headed for the scree. He obviously intended to trust to luck and slide down. Brogan was up on his feet and ran to the edge of the drop, took a steady aim and fired.

It was quite impossible to tell if he had hit Edwards or not as he did not stop rolling until he reached the bottom. When he did stop, he did not move and was quickly covered in loose rock rolling on top of him. Brogan stood and watched for some time before being satisfied that Edwards was, at the very least, badly injured. He turned to look at the old man and the lepers, who had now gathered outside the caves.

'What happened to the other two?' he asked.

'They are dead,' replied the leading leper, simply.

'Then I guess you don't need me no more,' said Brogan.

'There is still one man,' reminded the old man. 'The deputy was not among them. He will return and tell the sheriff what has happened. The army will still come.'

'I'll talk to him,' said Brogan. 'He seems a reasonable man.'

Brogan helped the deputy to load the bodies of the two white men across their horses. It was impossible to tell if it had been Brogan's shot or the fall which had killed Edwards. That was a decision which was to be left for the doctor to decide.

The deputy had, at first, insisted that the bodies of the two Indian policemen be brought out but he had changed his mind when, at Brogan's suggestion, he had seen the lepers. He had never seen anyone

stricken with leprosy before and had been plainly horrified when several of them had agreed to expose their rotting features. He was not prepared to risk taking back anyone whom he knew had been in direct contact with the lepers.

Of the twenty lepers, four had been killed and two injured, although not too seriously. Brogan had tried to talk the old man into leaving but his mind was set, he intended to remain and help look after the lepers.

'It is certain that I will become one of them,' he said. 'I do not mind, my wife and son are here and I am old. My time is almost here and I would like to die with my family.'

'Best of luck,' said Brogan. 'Maybe the others will come back and help.'

'Most of the old ways are gone,' said the old man. 'There are some ways and beliefs which will never die and fear of becoming one of the living dead is one of them. They will leave food as they always do but they will never look upon us'

'So what do you do now, Deputy?' asked Brogan.

'I collect the other bodies and take 'em back to Cottonwood,' replied the deputy. 'You ain't got nothin' to worry about though. You and Mary are both right about the way Indians are treated. As far as I'm concerned they all got killed takin' on those lepers, you weren't even here. I can't see nobody wantin' to come out here an' take 'em on either, not even the army.'

'I hope you're right,' said Brogan. 'I'd hate to think I wasted my time.'

'Like you said before, you did your best,' said the deputy. 'I still say that it ain't goin' to make a bit of difference though. There'll still be squaw hunters an' there'll still be the murder of Indians in these parts. The difference is that I intend to try an' do somethin' about it.'

'What about Jimmy Two Rivers?' asked Brogan. 'He's still got a price on his head. Won't they be out after him?'

The deputy smiled. 'There's at least two bodies back at the village with their faces shot to hell either one of which could be Two Rivers. It will be impossible for anyone to say who they really are so one of 'em might just as well be Jimmy Two Rivers. I can swear that I saw him killed.'

'You'd tell lies for the Indians?' asked Brogan.

'I'll tell lies for the sake of peace,' replied the deputy. 'I'll tell Mary about the lepers, I know she cares about things like that. She might have some idea if anythin' can be done for them. I'd like to think that there was.'

'Maybe there is,' said Brogan. 'I've seen lepers twice before an' on both occasion they were bein' looked after by monks an' nuns. I saw some monks back at Cottonwood, maybe they'll be prepared to look after them.'

'I'll talk to them,' agreed the deputy. 'Now, Mr Brogan McNally, get your ass out of here, out of this state an' out of my life before I change my mind and arrest you for murder. I hope I never see or hear of you again.'

'Are you tryin' to tell me I ain't welcome in California no more?' said Brogan with a laugh.

'That's exactly what I am sayin',' said the deputy. 'I ain't never seen you as far as anyone else is concerned. Now get your ass out of here.'

Brogan laughed, mounted his horse and turned away. 'You heard what the man said, old girl,' he said to her. 'Get your ass an' my ass out of here.'

The horse tossed her head, neighed and set off at a surprisingly brisk trot. Brogan did not look back, he never did; he hated saying goodbye.